STORY OF A MURDER

A Bookish Cafe Mystery Book 3

HARPER LIN

Story of a Murder

Copyright © 2021 by Harper Lin.

ISBN: 978-1-987859-87-4

www.harperlin.com

Chapter 1

The words to *"Yankee Doodle Dandy"* played on repeat in Maggie Bell's head as she stepped back to admire her latest creation for the Bookish Café's display window.

"I think you've outdone yourself, Mags," she said while standing a little straighter with pride.

Today was the hundredth anniversary of the establishment of Fair Haven, the place she'd called home for so long she could hardly remember anything else. But she couldn't recall seeing the town so alive and excited for the celebration as this year. Sure, the Fourth of July was always a big deal with fireworks and barbeques and people from all over visiting the quaint, quiet country before returning to Boston or wherever the hustle and bustle was. But this festival was especially for the folks of Fair Haven, the proud folks who took pride in their little metropolis and were happy to hear the mayor give a grand speech in the middle of town. After that, they'd line the streets for a parade, where the fire engines and police cars would flash their lights and blast their sirens as they tossed candy to the crowd.

Dogwood Grounds, the park not far from the Bookish Café, was filled with local vendors selling fresh honey, homemade soaps, hand-sewn quilts, and dozens of other delights. Maggie looked forward to exploring the booths during her lunch hour. The park also included people selling their antiques and vintage jewelry, and the night after this, there would be a display of old cars there that had the whole place abuzz.

Maggie knew nothing about cars, but from what Babs had told her, Roy would be showcasing his 1956 powder blue Chevy. Nothing was more important to some of the men in town as their old-fashioned cars. Babs was the bubbly assistant who worked on the café side of the Bookish Café. She was a blond bombshell who had quick wit and a smart remark for every occasion.

"You'd think those men had given birth to those

cars, the way they carry on," she said before flipping back one of her blond curls. She said the car show was such a big deal that the parking lot at the local grocery store was too small, and instead the Evangelical church was donating their spacious parking lot to the hot-rodders.

But down Main Street, every storefront was decorated in the most patriotic colors of them all, red, white, and blue.

Spotlight, the high-end clothing store, had glamorous red and blue dresses displayed on the mannequins in the windows. The beauty supply shop was as garish as always, featuring red, white, and blue hair extensions with matching fake eyelashes, blue and red lipstick, and a host of other oddball cosmetics that Maggie would never even consider wasting her money on. However, she was sure if she stepped into Tammy McCarthy's Bakery down the street, she'd find Tammy decked out with the patriotic fake lashes and half a dozen matching bows in her bright red hair. Those hair bows would also mirror the red, white, and blue sprinkles on some of her baked goods. Somehow, Tammy could pull it off and look as normal as if she was born into the world looking that way. If Maggie tried that look, she was positive she'd resemble Bozo the Clown.

The bank had tiny flags planted all around the property. Mr. Lorenze also had a tactful, solemn flag waving proudly in front of his funeral home. But no business looked as proud and elegant as the Bookish Café did, at least in Maggie's opinion.

Alexander Whitfield, who had been Maggie's employer and friend for years before he passed, had amassed a large arsenal of random trinkets and pictures over the years he'd been in business. In his desk, the storeroom, and the closets in the upstairs apartment lay a bounty of patriotic-looking fabrics, knick-knacks, and posters, and of course, there were books. Ultimately, the collection Maggie had displayed gave the impression that stepping into the Bookish Café was stepping back in time. She never really thought she'd enjoy decorating the store for the special occasions being celebrated around town. But as it turned out, she was a natural at it. More and more people would come in not only to look at her displays but to actually browse the books that Maggie had so carefully and meticulously arranged on the shelves.

As she put the finishing touches on her master-piece, she saw the growing number of folks peering in and waiting for the doors to be opened. Of course, she wanted to believe they were there to dive into the books and rich history of Fair Haven. In reality, the people were there for the café's coffee and pastries.

Still, Maggie was proud. Without wasting any more time, she looked at her watch. Then she walked confidently over to the door, snapped the lock back, and gave it a push.

"Good morning," she said. Greeting everyone was also something new for Maggie Bell. Her introverted nature had kept her rather isolated. Although she was yet to call herself a social butterfly, the fact she uttered a good morning to a group of strangers was as rare and unusual as spotting a yeti.

A few people smiled and gave her a "good morning" back. Some nodded, and others, as always, said nothing. Maggie always felt if she was willing to make an effort, they should be as well. Those individuals would get a stern look of scrutiny from Maggie and maybe, if she felt particularly bold, a slight eyeroll.

But this morning, she felt nothing would bother her. The window was done. The sun was shining outside. Casper, the stock boy, had already unpacked the boxes of new books that had arrived the previous afternoon. The day would be an easy one.

"Mags?" said a female voice from behind her. She'd seen a specific face among the crowd of morning visitors, but it didn't register. She'd recognized it, but it was part of a dream, wasn't it? That was a foggy remnant from something in her subconscious. It wasn't real. Was it?

Maggie turned around and saw the very real face of her half sister.

Chapter 2

"**A**ngel? What are you doing here?" Maggie asked.

"Good to see you too. Is that how you greet your baby sister?"

The young woman put her hand on her hip. Her belly button stared at Maggie from between a pair of cutoff jeans and a simple halter top. Silver rings with multicolored stones decorated most of Angel's fingers, and around her neck hung a delicate silver chain that looked all too familiar to Maggie. The charm was a silver teddy bear. Maggie had an identical charm that their father had given her. She didn't wear it, simply because it wasn't her style. She always thought her father should have known that, but he tended to pay much more attention to her sister. Maggie and Angel had an eight-year age difference, so the baby was allowed to be carefree and weird, especially when the baby was the polar opposite of the introverted bookworm that Maggie was.

"Well, it would have been helpful to know you were coming," Maggie said as she gave her sister a stiff-armed hug. Angel squeezed her tightly, making Maggie's voice go hoarse. "Did you bring the rest of your… group with you?"

Angel let go of Maggie and nervously tucked a few strands of hair behind her ears.

"I'm not with them anymore," Angel said.

"What's the matter? Not enough kale to go around? Did you find another crowd with a bigger compound—oh, wait, I mean commune—to spread out on?" Maggie snapped.

"It's not like that, Mags," Angel said. "Do you have to start with me the second I get here? It's like you've been waiting all this time, planning to unload on me."

"That would mean I was planning on you showing up here." Maggie pretended to look at a watch on her wrist. "I didn't know you were coming. Remember?"

"You're the only family I've got in the area,

Mags. Can't you not be mad at me, just until I get back on track?" Angel said with an eyeroll.

"I'm not mad at you, Angel. You're the youngest. You're supposed to be the one who does the dumb things," Maggie said.

"Yeah. I really did step in it this time, Mags. I should have listened to my big sister," Angel said just as Joshua Whitfield passed by.

If Maggie didn't already have a reason to be annoyed with Angel showing up unannounced, she certainly had one when she saw Joshua's reaction to her. He stopped so quickly she was sure he'd given himself whiplash.

"Did I hear that right?" he said as he looked the pretty stranger up and down and then looked at Maggie. "Sister?"

"Joshua Whitfield, this is my half sister, Angel Bell. Angel, this is Joshua, my boss." Maggie looked all over the room as she tried to avoid seeing Joshua's reaction. She knew exactly what it would be. He'd be smitten with Angel just like the boys always were, and she'd eat it up as if no man had ever talked to her in her life.

"It's nice to meet you," Angel said as she shook his hand and smiled.

"Well, I hope you don't mind my saying, but I

don't think there could be two women more oppo-site than you ladies. Wow," Joshua said, making Maggie's blood pressure rise.

"We get that all the time," she said.

"We do," Angel concurred.

"What are you doing in town?" Joshua asked.

"I came to visit and spend some time with Mags. We haven't seen each other in a long time. We need to do a lot of catching up, and I was hoping Mags would show me around town. It looks like everyone is planning for a big party," Angel said and looked at Maggie as if hoping she'd go along with the story. Maggie wanted to tell her sister to go pound sand. It wasn't that she hated her. She just didn't know her at all. It was like having a stranger ask for a personal tour of your life.

"Yeah. You might have a hard time finding a hotel room," Maggie said, not realizing how rude she sounded.

Angel chuckled and looked at Joshua, who looked at Maggie. "Maggie, you've got room at your house, don't you? Don't be silly, Angel. She's just teasing. You don't need to look for a hotel," Joshua offered.

Maggie glared at him.

"We'll work something out," Maggie said diplomatically. The last thing she wanted to do was show her real emotions and start screaming at her half sister like she had the last time they saw each other, almost four years ago.

"How can you just up and leave? Let me guess, there's a guy involved," Maggie had hissed.

"He's not just a guy. He's my soul mate," Angel replied. "You wouldn't understand, Mags."

"Soul mate? Are you serious? What the heck does that even mean?" Maggie scoffed.

"He's who I was made for," Angel replied. "Together we make a perfect unit."

"Unit?"

"Being. We're just perfect for each other. He makes me happy, Mags. Don't I deserve to be happy?"

"Not when it breaks our father's heart and leaves me all by myself," Maggie replied.

"Yeah, right. Maggie, you are the last person who needs anyone. All your life you've been alone, and you make it very clear that you like it that way," Angel snapped back.

"What happens every time I try to reach out to you or anyone for that matter? Remember, Angel? You and your little group of friends had quite a few laughs over your half sister talking about the job she took at the bookstore, didn't you? As soon as I left the room, that soul mate of yours said what? What did he say?" Maggie snapped.

"You weren't supposed to hear that," Angel said, looking down at the ground.

"He said I was already as dried up as the books I'd be selling," Maggie said sternly. "I didn't care what he thought of me. But then you laughed. You laughed along with him," Maggie's voice trembled, and her eyes filled with tears, but she quickly choked them back.

"It was just a joke. Echo didn't mean anything by it. He was just joking around," Angel pleaded. "It's not like you made him or any of my friends feel welcome. Heck, you didn't even make me feel welcome."

"Sure, *I* didn't. Maybe that was because I knew you were making a mistake. Maybe it's because I do care about you, and for once someone needs to ignore your feelings and tell you that this is not a commune but a cult, and it is wrong. Don't you see what they are asking you to do? To leave your family?" Maggie shook her head and crossed her arms.

"Only because no one supports me. You aren't supporting me!"

"My gosh, Angel! Since when does support

require I hand you the rope to hang yourself with?" Maggie shouted.

That was the last thing she said to Angel. Her sister turned her back and left, climbing into a Jeep with some dude with long hair and a goatee. Her new family was called the Great Society of Atonement. They were a group of what Maggie called numbskulls who loitered around young people's hangouts like the college grounds, bars, and coffeehouses for an opportunity to blow smoke then sweep them into the fold.

She'd never admit it, but when Angel left, Maggie cried. She was all alone and had only just started working for Mr. Whitfield. No one else would have noticed the difference, but Mr. Whitfield picked up on her sorrow almost immediately. He was the only person in Fair Haven who knew Maggie even had a sister. Up until now.

"Hey, I think I've got room upstairs," Joshua said, snapping Maggie back into the present.

"Oh my gosh, no. She'll stay with me," Maggie quickly replied. "I'll give you my address. It's easy to get to, and I've... got... room." The words felt clunky tumbling out of her mouth. Going home to a quiet house was one of Maggie's most favorite parts of the day. All of this went against the grain.

"Thanks, Mags. Since you are working, I'm going to go and take in some of the local flavors. What time do you get off work?" Angel asked as if they'd never uttered a cross word in their whole lives.

"I'll be done around five. Here." Maggie reached in her pocket and pulled out her keys. She removed one of them from the chain and handed it to Angel. "This is my house key in case you get tired. If I find out anyone other than you was in my house, you will be finding new accommodations. I don't…"

"I get it." Angel rolled her eyes then smiled at Joshua. "Get all the boys and beer out before you get home. Understood."

"The sarcasm certainly runs in the family," Joshua chuckled.

"Yeah, it's a family tradition," Maggie said with a smirk before stepping to the counter to write down her address. She handed the scrap of paper to Angel and pinched her lips together. Angel stuffed it into the back pocket of her shorts. She strung the key onto the silver chain around her neck, fastened it, and then touched it gently.

"I'll see you tonight," Angel said. "It was nice meeting you, Joshua."

"You, too, Angel." Joshua's smile made him look like a big, dopey hound to Maggie. It was her turn to roll her eyes. With a jingle of the bells over the door, Angel was gone, and Maggie groaned.

"Your sister seems really nice. What's the matter?" Joshua asked as he walked to the closed door to watch Angel walk away.

"We have nothing in common. Nothing," Maggie said as she straightened her blouse and proceeded to dive into her work. She had enough to keep her busy, and a few customers had books in their hands as they scanned the shelves. She'd wait at the counter to ring them up and decided not to look at Joshua.

"I'm sure you've got more in common than you think. You just haven't seen her in a while. How long has it…"

"Four years. I haven't seen her in four years, and she's eight years younger than me. And she's lived a totally different kind of existence from me. I just wonder why she's here."

"Maybe she just wants to see her sister?" Joshua was trying to be kind, but Maggie knew Angel enough to understand she had a reason to just show up. It wasn't like her to come seeking out approval or help.

"Yeah, maybe." Maggie forced an awkward, crooked smile and nodded. Maybe Joshua was right. But still, he hadn't been there the day Angel left. He hadn't heard her nonsense about the Great Society of Atonement. Sounded like the name a bunch of Goth kids would give their little clique. Fortunately, one of the customers who had been collecting books from almost every aisle came to the register, and she had to tend to him. Joshua smiled and went back to his work on the café side.

Maggie ran up the customer's purchases and was sorry to see Brian Kilmeade's *The Pirates of Tripoli* leave the store. She'd wanted to read that one. The coffee table book of Matisse was also one she'd looked through a dozen times and hated to part with. But from the looks of the man buying them, she was sure they were getting a good home. Still, Maggie would have liked a couple of additional days to have them to herself.

Chapter 3

"Surprise! Did you miss me?" Angel said just as Maggie was about to lock the store's front door. To be honest, Maggie felt like the girl hadn't left. She'd been on her mind all day.

"Did you have fun today?" Maggie asked as a yawn seized her.

"I did. There are some amazing little vendors at the park. I bought you something," Angel said, holding out a plain paper bag proudly. "Don't you just love this crinkly kind of bag? It makes such a comforting sound, like whatever is inside is a real treasure. There's no Hope Diamond in there, so don't get too excited."

Maggie, who had always thought the same thing

about this particular texture, took the bag. She smiled. "You didn't have to buy me anything. You should be saving your money for... gas or rent."

"Subtle." Angel huffed and rolled her eyes again.

Maggie smirked and opened the bag. The scent hit her immediately. When she looked inside, she saw a bar of white soap with tiny green flecks in it.

"Is this...?"

"Basil. Yes. Doesn't it smell like heaven?" Angel said.

"Oh my gosh, it does." Maggie stuffed her nose inside the bag and inhaled deeply then offered it to Angel, who did the same.

"I know it isn't a lot. I remembered you always liked the smell of fresh basil. I couldn't pass it up. And I have a little bit of money. It's no big deal. The least I can do, really. I know my showing up here has thrown a wrench into your daily existence. I really didn't have anywhere to go, Mags. Nowhere." Maggie watched, sure her sister's eyes and the tip of her nose reddened.

"What happened, Angel?" Maggie frowned in concern.

"I really tried to make it work," she said. "At first, I don't think I was ever happier. There was so much work to do, and everyone chipped in. It really was something beautiful to see. Mags, we had a garden that could feed this entire town. We made beautiful things to sell and built simple homes. You could walk out of one and into another if you felt like it."

Maggie pulled her chin into her neck when she heard that.

"I know you think it sounds strange, but it was no different from me walking into your room when we were younger. It was a real feeling of family," Angel said.

"You had a family already." Maggie couldn't stop the words.

"Not like this, Mags. I wasn't just sitting around watching television in a nice house wasting away before I even experienced anything," Angel replied.

"Right, because that was what we did. We watched television all the time." Maggie rolled her eyes. "I don't know what makes me angrier, Angel. The fact that you left or the fact that you thought you had it so bad."

Angel pinched her lips together. "It was good there, Mags. Not until I'd been there about a year. Then things got bad. Really bad."

For the first time since her arrival, Maggie saw

Angel not as her flaky sister but as a woman. A shadow fell over Angel's face. Her usual confident, carefree look vanished. Angel looked scared. Plain and simple.

"Okay, let's get out of here and…" Just then, there was a knock on the glass door, and another familiar face from Maggie's past peeked in between the backwards lettering that spelled out the words Bookish and Café.

"Oh, no." Angel sighed.

"Is that…?"

"Yes," Angel sighed.

"He's looking for you, I assume," Maggie said as she walked over to the door and snapped the lock back. Angel said nothing as Maggie pulled the door open.

"Hi," the man said. He was tall, wearing a white T-shirt and jeans with flip-flops and a couple of bizarre bracelets around both wrists. Maggie never liked jewelry on men. Occasionally, a gold chain around the neck looked kind of sexy, but even that was rare. Black rubber rings or braided hemp bracelets on a grown man were even sillier.

"Echo?" Maggie asked, looking as if she'd just bit into a soup grape.

"Yeah, how did you know?" he asked.

"Sharp as a tack, Angel," Maggie said as she stepped aside to let her sister converse with her boyfriend. But that wasn't what happened at all. The two did not reunite. Although Echo seemed relieved and happy to see Angel, the look on Angel's face made Maggie wish she hadn't opened the door.

"Stay away from me!" Angel shouted. And then things got loud.

Chapter 4

"Angel, you don't mean that," Echo said as he stepped in front of Maggie.

"Yes, I do! If you don't get away from me, my sister is going to call the police!" Angel shouted, getting the attention of Joshua and Babs from the café. Even Casper, who had been quietly stocking the shelves in the storeroom, came out to see what was going on.

Echo turned and looked at Maggie. He had wide green eyes, and his hair fell over his forehead in a way that some women, like Angel, would find alluring. Maggie wished for a pair of scissors to cut the unruly locks from his head.

"Maggie?" Echo said in a voice as smooth as velvet. "Wow. You've changed."

"No. No I really haven't. Echo, we're closing and…"

"Yes. Of course. Angel, come on. I'll take you home," Echo said and extended his hand. Angel recoiled like he'd offered her a claw.

"I'm not going anywhere with you. Not now. Not ever again," Angel hissed.

"Echo, I think you need to just go," Maggie said. She didn't like conflict and was never the kind of person to step into a fight between two other people. But these weren't just two random people. One of them was Angel.

"Maggie, your sister doesn't know what she's saying. You know how easily influenced she is. She needs to come with me," Echo replied. He was right about Angel being easily influenced.

"No, I don't!" Angel shouted as she took a few steps back.

"She doesn't want to, Echo. Just go and when things cool off, you can talk it over. I'm sure…" Maggie started.

"Angel! Stop this! You know you have to come with me! Stop doing this! Stop hurting me!" Echo shouted, his face turning red and his eyes bulging from their sockets. He looked like a totally different person. A Jekyll and Hyde for sure. The boom of his voice not only made Maggie and Angel jump but brought Joshua into the mix.

"Hurting *you*?" Angel shot back.

"You are everything to me, Angel. Please. Everyone misses you. Not just me. Everyone. Lucas and Sunshine and Palmer. What will I tell them? How do you think they'll feel knowing you just abandoned them?"

Maggie's eyes popped open, and she looked at her sister. "Do you have children?"

"What? No! Those are the Advisors. That's what they like to call themselves. I don't really care what you tell them. I'm not a cow, Echo. You don't own me."

"Angel, you don't know what you're saying." Echo tried to soothe her, but she backed up again when he reached for her.

"That's close enough, Echo. If you lay a finger on me, I swear you'll draw back a stump!"

"Angel! I love you! I've never loved anyone like I've loved you! It can be so perfect if you'll just come with me!" Echo sobbed and cried out.

"I'll kill you if you come near me again!" Angel shouted.

"All right! That's enough. Sir, I'm going to have to ask you to leave," Joshua said and stood in between Angel and Echo. Before anyone could say or do anything, Angel ran to the back room. Maggie heard the back door open and slam shut.

"Oh, no. Did she leave?" Echo sniveled.

"Sounds that way," Maggie replied. "I think it was pretty clear she didn't want to talk to you. Maybe you should just go home and wait until she's cooled off."

"I'll get her back. I have to." Echo looked at Maggie. Tears rolled down his cheeks.

Maggie felt uncomfortable watching the man blubber all over himself. It was like she was walking a dog that decided to poop just as a group of people were walking by. She was embarrassed for him.

"Men shouldn't cry in public. Really," she said and took a paper napkin from behind the counter and handed it to him.

"I'm sorry. I'm so sorry," he continued and looked at Maggie. "You have to help me."

"Who? What? Me? No. I don't get involved in my sister's business," Maggie said, wrinkling her nose like the whole thing smelled bad.

"I'm begging you," Echo continued and tried to step past Joshua like he wasn't even there. But Joshua wasn't impressed with Echo's display of emotions either.

"Sir, we are closed. I'm going to have to ask you to leave now," Joshua said, not moving an inch.

Maggie couldn't help it. She was glad Joshua was there and taking the reins. Especially when she saw how Echo's eyes snapped in his direction like he was not only surprised Joshua was there but that he spoke.

"Oh, you're closed. You're closed." Echo clenched his hands nervously before nodding and making his hair bounce. "I see."

Maggie quickly stepped to the door and held it open for him. She wondered if he remembered her and what he'd said all about her those few years ago. Were there any feelings of regret or embarrassment?

"Maggie, you have to help me. You have to help me get her back," Echo said before stepping out.

She hadn't realized it before, but now that she was close to him, she could smell him. The smell wasn't the most horrible she'd ever experienced, but it was a definitely a strange funk. What were those hippies at the Great Society of the Atonement eating? Or maybe Echo was the last to use the communal bath water and doused himself with some homemade cologne instead.

"If she wants to talk to you, she'll talk to you,"

Maggie replied while remaining safely behind Joshua.

"You don't know how much I love her. I just need a few minutes alone with her. Then she'll tell you how much we're in love. We just had a misunderstanding. That's all. My gosh, I'd walk through fire for her, and she knows it," Echo said as he wiped his eyes. "When I look up at the sky at night, the stars twinkle just for us. Ever since the first day I looked into her eyes I knew we were soul mates."

There was that stupid phrase again. For a few seconds Maggie thought that maybe, just maybe Echo was really, truly that in love with her sister. Walking through fire and staring at the stars was all very romantic. Then he had to go a ruin it with a trendy term like *soul mates*.

"Yeah, okay. I'll be sure to tell her that," Maggie said as Joshua carefully but deliberately pushed the door shut and snapped the lock in place.

"That's dangerous," Babs said. She'd been watching from the door joining the café to the bookstore and wringing a towel in her hands.

"What is?" Joshua asked.

"That man's behavior," Babs said. "I had a guy acting almost just like that right before I met Roy. It didn't end well. Does your sister know any bouncers or ex-military?"

"No. Why?" Maggie asked.

"Because a man like that will only stop when a couple of dudes bigger than him with a fondness for beating people up step into the picture," Babs replied.

Casper, Joshua, and Maggie looked at her and then one another. None of them could even pretend to be that kind of man. As if she was reading their minds, Babs spoke.

"It's okay. I'll get Roy and a couple of his grade-school buddies, and they'll pay him a visit for your sister. I know they'll handle…"

"No, Babs. That's really sweet," Maggie said. "I just don't think it will be necessary. If there is one thing about *Angel*, she isn't one. She knows how to handle herself. I'll talk to her tonight."

"Okay, but if you change your mind, just let me know," Babs said before pouting her bright red lips and batting her thick black lashes.

Maggie looked at Joshua, who got up close to the glass door. "He's gone. I think Maggie is right. Angel seems like a smart girl who can handle herself," he said before focusing on Maggie. "If anything happens, you don't hesitate to get the police over to your place."

"Look, nothing is going to happen. He's probably coming down from a bad trip and freaking out a little. Whatever happened between him and my sister will probably be patched up tomorrow before lunchtime," Maggie said, even though she wasn't sure.

The last thing she knew about her sister was what her romantic life was like. She'd also never known her sister to do any kind of drugs or associate with anyone who did. However, drugs were the only thing that could explain Echo's strange behavior. Either that or he was just a jerk. Maggie would talk to her sister about it when she got home. At least that was her plan.

But when she got there, Angel was nowhere to be found.

Chapter 5

The sun had set hours ago, and Angel still had not shown up at Maggie's house. A ruckus had occurred outside her back door. When she yanked the door open with a butcher knife in her hand, ready to do battle, she yelped to see Mrs. Peacock holding up a pitchfork to defend herself.

"Maggie, you scared the daylights out of me! Goodness, put down that knife. When you are dealing with weaponry, girl, please utilize something you can actually handle, like a broom. Do you really think you could stab someone?" Mrs. Peacock huffed as she pushed her hair up and away from her forehead.

"Sorry. It was my first instinct," Maggie said

and quickly set the knife down on the kitchen counter. As much as she hated to admit it, Mrs. Peacock was right. She'd never be able to stab someone. The idea was gross enough, let alone actually committing the act. "What are you doing back here?"

"We've got moles," Mrs. Peacock replied. "I am positive that Mrs. Donovan had them first and somehow managed to chase them into my beautiful yard. She knows how strapped I am for money and that I'm on a fixed income. It will cost me a fortune to hire someone to exterminate them. This is so Mrs. Donovan can say I have moles. As if the old biddy doesn't have more moles on her saggy chins than I'll ever have in my yard."

"Moles?" Maggie asked and looked at the ground.

"I saw the little devil beneath the ground and was just about to stick him when you decided to make an appearance. Oh, this is terrible. I'm sure he's gotten away," Mrs. Peacock said with a huff.

"You were going to stab it with that pitchfork?"

"Yes, honey. I can't very well let the thing go on and terrorize my garden from below. Then Mrs. Donovan will take the title for best lawn in our subdivision. That reminds me, Maggie. Please pull the weeds in front of your house and in the flower-pots. I think I saw a couple," Mrs. Peacock said before looking down at the ground for movement.

"It's good to know you can stab someone if you need to." Maggie wrinkled her nose.

"Don't you forget it." Mrs. Peacock smirked.

Maggie was one of the few people who knew Mrs. Peacock wasn't exactly as she appeared. It didn't surprise her one bit that the woman was willing to kill a rodent with a pitchfork while wearing one of her flowing silk muumuus and sparkly slippers.

"Do you need any help?" Maggie asked.

"No. I'm sure the beast has run off for now," Mrs. Peacock replied, her free hand on her hip. "Don't forget about those weeds."

"Yes, ma'am," Maggie answered respectfully. "My sister might be stopping by tonight."

"Your sister? I didn't know you had a sister." Mrs. Peacock huffed again. "How long will she be staying? You know this is a single-bedroom house. It's not made for large crowds to accommodate."

"She's only going to spend the night. Maybe two," Maggie replied, trying to convince herself that was going to be the case. She really had no idea how long her sister was planning on staying in town. That made her even more jittery than she had been waiting for her to show up. Angel had stormed out of the bookshop, and Maggie hadn't heard from her. Plus, Maggie hardly considered her sister staying a couple of nights as *a large crowd*.

"I suppose that will be all right," Mrs. Peacock said.

"Thanks," Maggie said.

"Well, no use standing out here for nothing. That mole has probably tunneled all the way to Hickory Creek by now. Pity," Mrs. Peacock slung her pitchfork over her shoulder and headed back toward the house.

"Sorry," Maggie replied.

"Good night, dear."

"Good night, Mrs. Peacock, and thanks again," Maggie said and received a wave in return.

While she was out, Maggie walked to the front of the house. The small lamp on the front porch gave off a warm glow. Crouching down, she looked along the front of the house and found one stray weed sprouting up from the ground and two more in one of the pots. That was enough to drive Mrs. Peacock crazy. The daisies and marigolds were in full bloom and looked as pretty as they always did. They made a simple display of flowers around

Maggie's little house on Mrs. Peacock's property. Meanwhile, Mrs. Peacock's house was surrounded by an oasis of every color imaginable. She tended quite a bit of it herself and had won the coveted Fair Haven Yard Beautification Award for her efforts for the past few years. The rivalry between her and Mrs. Donovan for the prettiest lawn, the best Christmas decorations, and the most bountiful garden had not only gone on for years but become a main attraction in itself.

Maggie did her part to help her landlady. The last thing she wanted was for the woman to blame her for losing the award. But she didn't expect to find what she did among the daisies.

"Mags," Angel whispered and sniffled, making Maggie yelp and then clamp her hand over her own mouth.

"Jeez, Angel. What are you doing in the flowers?" Maggie reached her hand down to help her sister stand up.

"I didn't want that woman to see me." She wiped her nose on the back of her hand.

"Angel! What happened to you?" Maggie hissed so as not to alert Mrs. Peacock.

"Can we go inside?" Angel began to sob.

"Of course." Maggie put her arm around her

sister's waist and led her into the house. She shut the door and locked it tight.

"I'm so sorry about this," Angel said.

"Just go into the kitchen. I'll make us some tea," Maggie replied before closing her curtains too. When she walked into the kitchen, her heart broke as Angel begged to leave the light off.

Maggie could tell she was soaked and thought it looked like she'd rolled around in dirt. Her hair was a mess, and her eyes were red and puffy from crying.

"This isn't what I wanted to have happen," Angel started as she sat at the kitchen table.

"What happened?" Maggie asked, staring at her sister. Something inside Maggie shifted. She felt it like something snapped in place or a switch was flipped. Regardless of the circumstances, Maggie was taking Angel's side.

"I'm so ashamed," Angel replied.

Maggie took a deep breath and sat down at the kitchen table. The only light came from a small nightlight over the counter that gave off a warm glow. Maggie didn't comfort her sister. This wasn't the time. What Maggie wanted was the truth. "What happened?"

"It wasn't like this from the beginning, Mags. I

swear. Something happened to Echo, to half the people at the GSA. I don't know when exactly. It seemed like everything was going along fine. Like I said, we were thriving, living as a real community," Angel said then swallowed hard. "Things were amazing…until they weren't."

Angel went on to describe her life at the Great Society of Atonement community. They had a building where everyone had a room to call their own.

"It wasn't a lot, but we'd all decided we didn't need a lot. Just a roof over our heads and a bed to sleep in. I'd pick wildflowers and keep them in a vase, and there were a couple of books I kept."

"Let me guess. *The Scarlet Letter* and *House of the Seven Gables*," Maggie replied with a smirk.

"That's your fault." Angel smiled. "I would have never read Hawthorne if you didn't make his books sound so good when you were in high school. The scandal that was in both of them was just shocking for the days it was written in."

"Very risqué. I knew if I mentioned that and told you the topics weren't appropriate for your age, you'd be all over them. I was right," Maggie teased, happy to see a slight smile on Angel's face. But it disappeared quickly.

"We all had tasks that we rotated. There was a small, tightknit group of us. It wasn't until the founder showed up that things started to change. Grisham. Slowly at first. Echo was given more responsibility. Strange responsibilities like running errands late at night and kind of acting like a police officer. We used to talk about our future together. You know, kids and a house. Then, he stopped talking about that stuff and would only talk about what Grisham had said to him that day," Angel said just as the kettle went off. Maggie got up, poured two cups of peppermint tea, and placed them on the table before resuming her seat.

"Who is Grisham? Does he have a last name or is he too cool like Madonna or Cher?"

"I'm surprised you know who Madonna and Cher are," Angel chortled in between tears. "He's the leader. He started the GSA in California or Oregon or something. At least, that was what I was told. I wondered how true that was because the guy was rather stupid and had very little personality. His right-hand man was who really appeared to be running the show," Angel said before taking a sip of her hot tea.

"But you were happy there?" Maggie asked.

"At first. But like I said, things started to change.

It was like Grisham and his entourage had a plan in mind to tear everyone down and rebuild them almost backwards from where they had been. Just for example, they wanted me to go into town and get some supplies. But they didn't give me any money. I was supposed to prove myself by stealing," Angel replied. "I never could do it. You and I were raised differently because of our ages. I know that, Mags. But we were taught you don't steal. It's a pretty basic thing to teach your kids, right?"

Maggie nodded her head and took a sip of tea but didn't speak.

"I decided to just use my own money. I had a good bit saved up and figured there would be no harm in that. It was mine. I could do with it what I wanted and if I wanted to spend my money on our community to keep us safe, well, I was going to do that. Besides, it was flour and oil and the things we couldn't grow ourselves." Angel took a sip of tea. Maggie noticed her hands begin to shake.

"But then they found out what I was doing. The only one I told about the money was Echo. He was the only one. And when I confronted him when we were alone, he laughed at me. He said that he had to do it in order for me to grow. To become a better woman. That it was all some kind of test and I flunked because I was still stuck to 'Daddy' and 'Big Sis.'" Angel's eyes filled with tears.

"You left when you were twenty-two. Why didn't you just come back? Sure, you would have gotten an *I-told-you-so*, but you'd have been home." Maggie shook her head.

"It didn't happen overnight, Mags. That place was my home. For the first six months it was all I ever dreamed it could be. I felt grown up. I felt like I was making a difference. But nothing I did was right. Everything was wrong. Do you know how it feels to be reminded every day that you aren't good enough? That you aren't working hard enough? That you aren't pretty enough anymore? Not smart? Not contributing? That you are an embarrassment? I never knew what a failure I was until Grisham showed up and told Echo."

She finally broke down in uncontrollable sobs.

Maggie was paralyzed. She didn't hug people. She didn't pat their heads and soothe their hair when they were upset. It wasn't her style. But this was her half sister. They shared the same blood. So, she did the most comforting thing she could. She took Angel's hand and gripped it.

Maggie swallowed hard, squared her shoulders, and cleared her throat. "Okay. You are here now.

You are safe. Tomorrow, we'll go talk to Gary Brookes. He's the deputy here and…"

"Gary Brookes? Didn't you and he go to high school?" Angel sniffed and managed a little smile when Maggie nodded. "I remember him. He was always sweet on you."

"What? Gary? You've obviously smoked some of that wacky tabacky that cults like to pass around." Maggie blushed.

"Now you are the one that sounds high. We didn't do things like that. No alcohol. No drugs. No romance. No music." Angel took a sip of tea. "We were supposed to celebrate hearing the beating of our own hearts."

Maggie wrinkled her nose. "Are you serious?"

Angel nodded her head and chuckled. "I know. It all seems so stupid now."

"It seemed stupid then. You just didn't know it," Maggie blurted out ,making Angel click her tongue before she chuckled again. "Like I was saying. Tomorrow we'll go to the police and…"

"No, Mags. No police. Please."

"Echo looked pretty convinced he wasn't leaving without you. I think we might need the help of the law," Maggie insisted.

"No. I don't want the law involved," Angel declared. "He's not going to try anything."

"We can't be too careful," Maggie said as she stood up and walked to the light switch. As soon as she flicked the light on, she gasped. "Angel? What happened to your clothes? Why are you all dirty? You look like you wrestled with a wild boar and..." Maggie gasped and put her hand to her lips as she tugged on Angel's wrist. "Are those bruises?"

"Margaret. I'm begging you. Don't involve the police. Believe me. It's over. Echo won't be bothering me anymore," Angel said, her eyes were hard in a way Maggie had never seen before.

"What did you do, Angel?"

"Nothing. Now please don't ask me any more questions. I'm so tired," Angel said.

"But if things got violent, Angel, you need to..."

"I just need to rest tonight. Please. We can talk about it tomorrow. I just need to rest," Angel replied before yawning wide.

Maggie nodded although she didn't really like the idea. But what would change between now and the morning? She gave Angel a pair of pajamas and told her to take a shower. Angel offered to sleep on the couch, but Maggie said no.

"We can share. Like we used to when we were kids," Maggie said, wrinkling her nose.

"Are you sure you don't mind?" Angel said, her nose also wrinkled.

"You can't sleep on that couch. It itches. I get the feeling you slept on the floor enough with the GSA. The only other option is we share," Maggie said as she crawled into her bed, ensuring she would at least get her favorite side.

"Thanks, Mags," Angel said with a wide yawn.

Maggie didn't say any more. She wanted to get up, call Gary right away, and tell him what had happened. But Angel asked for one night. It was the least she could give her. Angel had been through enough.

As Maggie lay there in the dark, her sister fast asleep beside her, she thought if she ever saw Echo again, she'd have more than a few choice words for him. She'd see him again, but any words she might have wanted to say would fall on deaf ears.

Chapter 6

When Maggie woke up, she realized she'd slept hard and deep without waking up once. That was rare. Usually a strange creak or a rustle outside would rouse her. She looked over and saw Angel still out cold, her mouth hanging open and her breathing steady and calm.

As quietly as possible, Maggie got up, got dressed and headed to work. She left a note for Angel telling her there were Pop-Tarts in the cupboard or oatmeal raisin cookies in the cookie jar. In the note, Maggie asked her sister to stay put and planned on calling her later to discuss what to do about Angel's situation. Maggie hated to admit it, but while she drove to work, she recoiled at the idea that her sister would stay with her for too much longer. It wasn't that she took up a lot of room. She didn't. But drama always followed Angel, and Maggie never could tolerate it. She was busy worrying about real life. She certainly didn't have time to dwell on the impact of American pipits on the mosquito population or other such nonsense that her sister deemed important. It wasn't that Angel was a flake. Well, she was. But her heart was always in the right place. The thought of her being told to steal, of being told she was worthless made Maggie's blood boil. If anyone was going to give Angel a hard time, it was her. And she'd never in a million years call her sister worthless or stupid. Strange? Maybe. A little weird? Absolutely. But Angel was a good person.

The more Maggie thought of it, the more she decided to get ahold of Gary immediately.

"As soon as I get to work, I'll call," she told the steering wheel of her car. "It won't be the first time Angie is mad at me."

Maggie didn't have to call. As soon as she unlocked the bookstore door and slipped inside, Gary and Joshua were there from the café side, each holding a steaming cup of java and chatting away.

She was shocked at how the two of them were

behaving. Normally, they had a bit of an edge between them, like any minute they would drop to the floor to see who could do more push-ups. But right now, they were acting like two boys who stumbled across the word "boob" in the dictionary but didn't read the definition.

"Hi?" Maggie squinted.

"Is your sister coming in?" Gary asked. "I don't think I even remember what she looks like."

"You can't forget her now," Joshua said. He took a sip of coffee and winked at Maggie. "Although you'd never suspect they were sisters. Night and day."

Maggie rolled her eyes and walked behind the counter, where she dropped her purse and was happily distracted for a few moments by Poe's neediness and purring.

"Don't you guys have something better to do?" Maggie asked.

"Well, is she coming by today?" Gary asked.

"I don't know. When I left her at home, she was still sleeping. Gary, can I talk to you for just a second?" Maggie asked.

"Yes, ma'am," Gary said pleasantly and sauntered up to her. Joshua was a step behind him.

"Alone?" Maggie said as she stood on tiptoe and looked at Joshua.

"I'm going." Joshua shrugged before he turned and walked back into the cafe. "Sheesh."

"You know I'm just teasing you. You'll always be the only Bell girl for…"

"Gary, I need to talk to you about my sister." Maggie waved her hand in front of her face as if she were shooing a fly. "It's serious."

"Okay, let me…" Just then, Gary's radio went off.

"Brookes, you there?" the dispatcher said in her scratchy voice.

"Yeah, Gloria. What's up?"

"Gary, we've got a 10-100 at the base of Hickory Creek Bridge," she said.

"Copy that. I'm on my way. 10-4," Gary said. "Sorry Maggie, we'll have to talk later."

"What's a 10-100?" Maggie asked. "Can it just wait a few minutes?"

"Technically, I'm sure it could, but it really wouldn't be right. A 10-100 is a dead body," Gary said. He turned and quickly left the bookstore.

Maggie forgot about Angel for a few minutes. A dead body at the base of Hickory Creek Bridge? That news would be all over town before tomorrow.

Heck, it would probably be the talk of the neighborhood by noon.

Maggie scratched Poe, who had made himself comfortable in a square of sunshine on the window ledge. It was a regular morning with a good number of window shoppers admiring Maggie's display window and then coming in. The café was bustling with people in the early-morning rush. Maggie could hear Babs's good-natured ribbing. In no time at all, Maggie got to know the regulars—and some who she would insist were *irregular*—and call them by name as soon as they walked in the door. That went on all morning. Before long came lunchtime, and that rush made its way through the door for a midday boost of coffee and something sweet to wash it down with.

Just as a couple of women approached Maggie at the counter with a copy of the latest best-seller that she had opposed but that Joshua had insisted they stock, Ruby Sinclair strolled into the bookstore. Her long, thin neck showed above a high, frilly cream-colored lace collar. She wore a long skirt, like a Victorian lady, and used a dainty black parasol as a walking cane. Her shoes were worn and dirty because she made this same walk almost every day.

The ladies at the counter looked at her and then

each other before stifling their giggles. Maggie knew Ruby. Rather, she knew her like the rest of the people in Fair Haven did. She was as tragic as the characters she used to play on stage before her father passed away. Mr. Sinclair adored his daughter and only child and did everything to make her happy. In return, she became a stage actress with a rather impressive resume. But when Mr. Sinclair died, something inside Ruby snapped.

She jiggled the doorknob three times before entering. Only Maggie noticed. Anyone else might have thought the peculiar woman just had trouble with the lock. Maggie knew it was her obsessive-compulsive disorder. It was why she always walked to the third row of books and tapped the top shelf three times. She never bought anything. Her mutterings Maggie couldn't understand most of the time. She wondered if they weren't lines from her plays.

"Is she in costume for the celebration?" one of the women at the counter asked.

"No," Maggie replied without offering any further explanation as she rang up their purchases. They left looking at Ruby and then each other and giggling again as they walked out.

"Good morning, Ruby," Maggie said as she went back to stroking Poe's fine black coat.

With her index finger up to her lips Ruby hurried to the edge of the aisle and looked at Maggie. Something always behind lay Ruby's eyes that made Maggie think she saw things no one else did.

"My father will hear about this," she whispered.

That was Ruby's catch phrase. Her father, in addition to adoring Ruby, also left her a sizable fortune that the spinster could never exhaust living the way she did. When he was still alive, if anything improper was going on, she would inform her dear old dad, who would step in when needed. She led a pampered life this way. Some people thought she was a tragic figure. Maggie envied her uniqueness and the way she just lived in *her* world. For all Maggie knew, it was absolute torture for her to roam the streets, muttering her lines from plays when the curtain had fallen long ago. But when she caught Maggie and said these words to her, she was sure the woman did have some joys in her life.

"You tell him, Ruby. I hope he does something about it," Maggie replied kindly and smiled.

"The bridge claimed another one," she whispered.

"Oh, the rumor of the body Gary went to investigate spread that fast, huh? Wow. I think that's a new record," Maggie said, shaking her head.

"My father will most definitely hear about this," Ruby said again before heading to the back exit, nearly running Casper down in her dramatic departure. Carrying a box of new releases, he quickly stepped out of her way, bowing his head in the process to give Ruby some extra theatrics for her exit. The back door slammed shut, and she was gone.

"What was that all about?" Casper asked as he put the box on the counter and then scratched Poe's head.

"Who knows. I guess she's already heard about the body," Maggie replied.

"What body?"

"The body at the base of Hickory Creek Bridge," Maggie said.

"What?" Casper gasped.

"Yeah, I guess it's all over by now. I only know about it because Gary was here when he got the call," Maggie said.

"I didn't hear anything about it. But no one really rushes up to tell me the latest gossip," Casper shrugged. "Hey, do you think Joshua would mind if

I left a little early today?"

"You'd have to ask." Maggie wrinkled her nose and looked up at the lanky youth. "What do you have to do?" she asked without any regard for his privacy. She didn't mean to sound bossy.

"I wanted to meet up with some kids and go hear the music they were going to be playing in the park," he said, his cheeks turning bright red.

"What are you blushing for?" Maggie asked like Casper had suddenly come down with a pimply, oozing rash.

"I'm not. It's j-just hot in here," he stuttered.

Suddenly Maggie realized that a girl was probably involved. She quickly switched gears and looked at the receipts she was going to have to deposit at the bank tonight.

"Oh. Yes. Well, I'm sure Joshua won't mind if you ask to leave a little early. Why don't you go ask him now? He's in the café with Babs. I think they are baking something new or brewing something new. I don't know," Maggie replied as awkwardly as Casper did.

After Casper left, she looked at her watch. She hadn't seen Angel all day and hoped she wasn't doing anything weird or getting in any trouble. There was only an hour left before quitting time, and she had no idea what she was going to cook for dinner. Maggie enjoyed frozen pizza or even a bowl of cereal. She was sure that Angel would be annoyed at the absence of tofu or wheat germ from the house. The thought of hearing a lecture about all the GMOs in her freezer made Maggie's head start to pound. She was probably going to hear it about her furniture not being made of hemp or her water coming straight from the tap without a filter.

"It's a small price to pay considering what she's been through," Maggie muttered just as the bells jingled over the door.

"Good afternoon, miss. Are you Margaret Bell?" a man with gray, slicked-back hair and wire-rimmed glasses asked.

"Yes," Maggie replied as her eyebrows instantly snapped into an angry position. She didn't like it when strangers knew her name. "Who are you?"

"Miss Bell, my name is Grisham. I'm looking for your beautiful sister. Is she around?" the man's teeth were perfectly straight, but one of his blue eyes hung lazily to the left.

"My sister? I haven't seen my sister in over two years." Maggie pinched her lips together.

"That's funny because her husband Echo was here yesterday, and he said he not only saw her but spoke to her and you as well. Now, do you want to tell me where she is? She needs to come home," Grisham stepped farther into the bookstore. He had a woman and two men with him. They didn't look like the hippies in old movies from the sixties. In fact, they looked like any people you might cross on a nature path or at a community garden theater. Their clothes were clean, and so were their hair and skin. Still, Maggie didn't see them as anything more than a squeaky-clean version of the Jim Jones cult. Of course, they may not have been that bad. But they were certainly weird.

And they took your sister, Maggie's conscience needled. She didn't want to admit how much she missed her baby sister. If she did, she'd just have to face that Angel would leave her again as soon as the next trendy group of smooth talkers showed up.

"Wait! Did you just say' husband'?" Maggie snapped out of her thoughts like she'd been dropped from an airplane.

"Yes. Echo and Angel had been one of our first couples to marry," Grisham said. "So you can see how important it is that she come back to us. We all miss her."

"Where is her husband now? I don't see him

here trying to win her heart back," Maggie snapped.

"We were hoping you might know that too. He went to meet with her last night and didn't make it back to the hotel," Grisham said. He stood innocently in front of her, his hands in his pockets.

"You're staying at a hotel? That's got to cost you a pretty penny. I thought everything was sold out because of the festival. Unless you knew you were going to be coming here," Maggie prodded.

"We find people are very generous when they are reasoned with. They don't want any bad publicity at a time like this," Grisham said.

"Why would any hotel in town get bad publicity for being sold out?" Maggie huffed. She didn't like where this was heading and suddenly wanted this group out of her bookstore. Maybe it wasn't technically *her* bookstore, but she certainly cared about it as if it were.

"Just because someone else made a reservation doesn't mean they need the rooms more than *we* do," Grisham said. "After all, we're searching for a missing woman. The wife of one of our members. Do you really think it would be prudent to leave us out in the street?" Grisham continued.

Once again, Maggie got hung up on that word

wife. She was a mess last night and had said that there would be no more problems with Echo. But if they were married, that threw a huge fly into the ointment. Had Maggie seen a wedding band or engagement ring on her sister's finger? She couldn't remember for sure. In fact, she thought she saw rings on all of Angel's fingers. It would be impossible to know if one of them meant *married* without asking her, and Maggie would ask her when she got home.

But additionally, Maggie didn't like Grisham's insinuation that he was willing to make a scene in a business to get what he wanted.

"Grisham, she's not here," said a third guy who Maggie hadn't even seen slip in. He was rail thin and deeply tanned with leather strap tied around his bicep. The second guy, who wore Birkenstocks with khakis and a crisp white T-shirt, whispered something to leather-bicep-strap-man that Maggie didn't hear. They both looked at her like she was the pork chops on sale at the butcher shop.

"Are you sure?" Grisham replied while still looking at Maggie.

"Yes. I think we should go back to the hotel and…"

"I think you need to remember who the head of this family is," Grisham growled.

"Hey, you were just *adopted* by this family. Not born into it. You don't have to let *his* crazy rub off." Maggie clamped her hand over her mouth only after all those words spilled out. She cleared her throat and smoothed her hair back before acting like she hadn't said a word. The entire group scowled at her, but no one made a move.

"I think maybe we should stay here until Angel shows up," Grisham said.

"I told you I haven't seen Angel. Just because you say some dude claiming to be her husband saw her that doesn't mean anything," Maggie said. "Besides, I don't know you from a hole in the ground. So maybe you should get a couple more facts straight before thinking I'd start handing over information on *my* family."

Grisham chuckled. "I can tell *you* are lost. Much like your sister was."

"And *is now*, since you can't find her?" Maggie needled. "Look. I know exactly where I am. I'm in the Bookish Café and Bookstore, and I'm getting ready to close up. So unless you are buying some books or going to get some coffee, you need to make your way to the door."

"If you'd just talk to me, Margaret, I'll bet you'd find we have a lot in common. Outsiders. Introverts. I know you just by looking at you, Margaret," Grisham said.

"Yeah. Okay. Time to go." Maggie looked out the window.

"Thank you for your time, Margaret. We'll be talking again soon," Grisham said.

Her mouth held a bitter taste as she watched the G.S.A. members leave. Grisham caught her eye, and Maggie found it very hard to look away. He had an intense, fiery, seductive look that made her feel like her slip or the lace of her bra was showing. Finally, she blinked and turned her attention toward some random book under the counter. Once they were gone and the bells had stopped jingling, Maggie walked over to the door and snapped the lock in place.

Chapter 7

A few minutes went by as Maggie counted the register and filled out all the paperwork, but she still felt the presence of the G.S.A. lingering around like the reek of patchouli. None of them smelled like the old scent of stoners, though. In fact, the G.S.A. people smelled clean and normal. Maybe that was the problem. They were a cult that didn't look like a cult. Maggie was sure that was what made them so dangerous. Combine the confusing appearance and the perplexing beliefs with Grisham's captivating stare, and Maggie was sure those were the main ingredients that captivated their followers.

As she was dissecting the entire group, she heard frantic knocking on the display window.

Maggie let out a yelp and glared at the face staring in at her. Angel chuckled.

"What is the matter with you, scaring me like that? Oh my gosh! Angel!" Maggie gasped when she saw the marks on her sister's neck and shoulder. "What happened to you? Did Echo do that to you?"

"It's nothing, Mags," Angel said with a nervous smile.

"I didn't see it last night or I would have called the police, no matter what you said," Maggie replied. "Why didn't you tell me?"

"I just didn't want to talk about it. I *don't* want to talk about it. Mags, it's never going to happen again," Angel replied.

"Right. How can you be so sure? A guy who does that once will do it again. They always do. Oh, Angel. I'm going to call Gary. You've got to tell him what happened and…" Maggie stopped speaking when Angel put her hand on her arm and squeezed.

"He won't ever touch me again, Mags. Don't make me say it anymore. Just believe me when I tell you he won't." Angel's eyes reddened and glistened with tears she was restraining.

Maggie tilted her head and blinked. She wanted

to hug her sister and slap her all at once. Instead, she took her hand and squeezed back.

"Oh, hello," Joshua said as he walked in from the café side. "It's really nice to see you again, Angel. What have you been up to?"

"Hi, Joshua. I went for a hike and ended up tripping over some tree roots. Gravity can be brutal," she tittered, rubbing her arm, which was also scraped up from the night before.

"That looks like it hurt," Joshua said.

"You should see the other guy." Angel winked and smiled making Joshua laugh while simultaneously making Maggie cringe.

It didn't help her nervous state when Gary walked in either. All she needed was another groupie for her flaky sister who was trying to hide that her "husband" had put his hands on her. But Gary's expression was all business. Maggie pursed her lips and squinted at him when she saw that the spell her sister usually cast had not taken hold.

"Hello, Officer Brookes," Joshua said. "Have you met Maggie's sister, Angel?"

"Oh, uh, hi. Angel?" Gary said forcing a smile as he reached out his hand to her. Maggie watched his eyes, waiting to see him give her a long once-over like Joshua did. But Gary did no such thing.

"What's the matter?" Maggie asked.

"I'm sorry to talk about such things in front of you, since we just met, but we found a body this morning. The only form of identification in his pocket was half a prescription. The other half was ruined by the water. His name was Echo Manns. He's not from town. According to the stuff we could make out the prescription was made in Boston. He had no money. No keys for a car or house. But one thing he did have was a huge gash on his head." Gary looked at everyone suspiciously. At least that was how Maggie saw it because all she could think of were the words Angel had said just a few minutes ago.

"He won't ever touch me again, Mags. Don't make me say it anymore. Just believe me when I tell you he won't."

When she looked at her sister out of the corner of her eye, Maggie was shocked to see no nervous expression or even the slightest twitch that indicated that she knew the deceased. This would be all Maggie needed. It never failed. Ever since they were kids, drama followed Angel around like a shadow. But still Maggie couldn't very well turn in her sister right then and there. No matter what, Angel was her family.

"Wow." Angel shook her head and clicked her tongue. "I'm sorry."

"What are you sorry for? You didn't do it," Gary said through a guffaw.

Maggie gasped then choked and coughed.

"Are you all right?" Angel asked.

"Yes," Maggie gurgled. "It just went down the wrong pipe."

"What did? The air?" Angel asked as she patted Maggie on the back.

"We had a couple reports of a guy fitting this description who was with a group. They were causing some problems with some of the local businesses," Gary said. "Did you guys have any trouble with any unfamiliar faces?"

Maggie wanted to tell him about the Great Society of Atonement members, especially Grisham, but out of the corner of her eye, she saw Angel slowly shaking her head.

"I don't think so." Maggie scrunched up her face and looked at Joshua. "Was there any trouble in the café?"

"Babs doesn't really tolerate trouble," Joshua said, rocking on his heels.

"Okay, good. That's the bad thing about these festivals sometimes. You don't have any way of knowing who the bad apples are. H.H. Holmes killed who knows how many people in Chicago in the 1893 because the World's Fair was taking place there. Who could keep track of all the visitors? No one," Gary said.

"That's a nice tidbit of the macabre to be rattling around in your head," Maggie said.

"I'm a fount of weird trivia and random sports facts," Gary replied with a smirk.

"Maybe someone in the group he was running with had something to do with his death," Angel said, making Maggie cough again.

"Do you need a glass of water?" Joshua asked. Maggie shook her head and waved her hands in front of her.

"She needs some fresh air," Angel said. Maggie nodded as she cleared her throat. She looked at her sister and took her by the hand before slinging her purse over her shoulder.

After getting her coughing under control, Maggie asked, "You don't need us for anything more, do you Gary?"

"No," Gary said.

Maggie quietly let out a deep breath and, without looking back, pulled Angel out of the bookstore. Once they were a few strides away from the front door, Maggie stopped and glared at Angel.

"*Now* what's wrong with you?" Angel asked.

"You know darn well what's wrong with me," Maggie said with a huff.

"You are attracted to that cop and won't do anything about it?" Angel asked, batting her long eyelashes. Even though her hair was a sandy brown and Maggie's was nearly black, her facial expressions mirrored Maggie's to a T.

"What? No! That's Gary and… no. What's… Oh, you are crazy!" Maggie felt her cheeks blaze and wanted to have a knock-down-drag-out shouting match with Angel like they'd had more than once when they were still living under the same roof.

"Ha! Could have fooled me. You are all relaxed, and you stand a little straighter and…"

Maggie grabbed Angel by the arm and pulled her into the doorway of the beauty supply shop to avoid being overheard. "Angel, that wasn't interest in anyone. That was freaking out that the guy who was beating on my sister suddenly showed up dead and not only were the police involved but my sister reassured me that he was nothing to worry about anymore. Fishy-fishy," Maggie pleaded.

"You think I killed Echo?"

"Angel, you didn't even flinch when Gary said it," Maggie hissed. "Did you do it?"

"If I said yes, what would you do?"

"That isn't the question, Angel. Please, tell me the truth. We'll figure out what to do together. I'll make sure you have a good lawyer and that the court knows what Echo did to you. It would be self-defense. No one would blame you and…"

"I can't believe you think I did this." Angel's expression broke Maggie's heart. All of a sudden she wasn't this beautiful young woman who was nothing more than a free spirit that never worried about tomorrow. Instead, she was the young girl who wanted to tag along with Maggie whenever she left the house to go to the library or for a walk alone.

"Can you blame me?" Maggie's words just tumbled out.

Angel looked at her. "There's a gypsy with a tent who is telling fortunes in the park. Do you want to go with me?"

"Are you serious?"

"Yes. Why wouldn't I be?"

"Angel, I think you need to tell Officer Brookes about your relationship with Echo. Being his wife isn't something that you can stop from bubbling to the surface," Maggie replied.

Angel blinked and took half a step back. "Where did you hear that?"

"Grisham came to the bookstore looking for you," Maggie said. "He told me you were Echo's wife. Do you know how stupid I felt hearing this news from him?"

"Not as stupid as me actually being Echo's wife," Angel scoffed.

Those words halted Maggie in her tracks. What had happened to Angel? There was obviously more to the story than what she was admitting to.

"Let's go home and talk this out. You have to tell me exactly what happened last night Angel. What you did. You have to," Maggie pleaded without raising her voice.

"I want to go see the psychic gypsy and see if she's got any good news for me," Angel said with a sad smile. "Then I want to go get a big bag of popcorn and hang around the park until everyone goes home. I want to talk about the stars and moon and clouds in the sky. I just want to admire what is beautiful for a while and not think about anything."

"How can you say that when your husband is dead?" Maggie didn't wrinkle her nose or squint.

She stared blankly at her sister like she was waiting for the right emotion to hit her and would then express herself. But it never came.

"It's because he's dead I can say these things. I'm sorry Mags. I think I'd rather be alone for a while," Angel said and lifted her chin just a little.

"Why don't you come home and…"

"I'll be home later," Angel said before she turned and hurried away from Maggie.

Seeing her leave that way made Maggie feel like the worst sister ever. Again, she watched her sister leave her just standing there. Part of her wanted to rush after her and take her hand like when they were younger. But another part of her was too terrified.

Maggie could not possibly ignore her sister's complete lack of empathy for the man she had claimed to love, to be her soul mate. The only other people who were able to distance themselves like this were the heavy hitters like Ted Bundy, Richard Ramirez the Night Stalker, and Aileen Wuornos. Could her sister have developed into this kind of person? A severe head injury could do the trick and turn a kind, gentle individual like her into a cold-blooded killer. The phenomenon was well documented. Science had made this connection a long time ago. Where the most horrific thought Maggie had ever conjured came from, she didn't know. But she wondered if Echo had given her sister a head injury. Her eyes welled with tears, and she was about to dart after Angel but realized while in her daydream, Angel had disappeared into the crowd.

Chapter 8

Angel had crept in the house through the open back door like she did so many times in their father's house when she and Maggie were younger. Maggie, who was almost always home, left the door open for Angel in case she missed curfew. The last thing Maggie wanted was for her sister to spend the night out in the garage or the shed, getting sick from the smell of gasoline or cleaning chemicals. The young girl, for all her wild ways, had never come home drunk or stoned. She just liked the night and being out in it. She never had any incidents with the police, at least not until now.

Maggie thought of getting up to talk to her about the days' events, but when she heard Angel let out a long sigh as she cozied up on the couch, she couldn't bring herself to go and disturb her. Something inside Maggie told her that Angel was enjoying the most peaceful rest she had gotten in a long time. Whether Angel killed Echo or not, Maggie wanted her to rest. In the morning, Maggie would ask her where she had gone, who she was with, and what she had done. For now, she'd let her off the hook.

But, as happened with most well laid-out plans, Angel was already gone when Maggie awoke. A note lay on the kitchen table.

"Gone to watch the sun rise. Will stop by the bookstore later. Sorry, ate the last banana.

-Love, Angel"

A big loopy heart and a smiley face sat under her name. "Where does she get so much energy?" Maggie huffed as a yawn crept up in her, stretching her mouth wide. She rubbed her face, pulled her hair back, and went to the bathroom to get ready for the day. When she tried to think of how to talk to Angel about her concerns, she drew a complete blank. The girl tended to just walk away from things she didn't like. Maggie had to make sure to get Angel in a place where she had no chance getting away. That would be hard.

Again, because of the influx of tourists, Maggie's usual parking spot was taken, forcing her to park nearly five blocks away. As she got out of her car, she could hear the familiar shouting from Patrick Cusic's garage. Metal clanged on the ground. An engine roared then died. A stream of obscenities followed. Maggie shivered. Not long ago, she had the displeasure of having to deal with Patrick Cusic, who some men said was the best mechanic in all of Fair Haven. He was a monster of a man who had the manners of an unchained junk-yard dog. Although he did fix her car at no charge, she was still terribly intimidated by the guy. No one normal reached a height of six and a half feet tall and a weight of over three hundred pounds. Without looking at the open garage door too closely, Maggie grabbed her bag from the passenger seat, slammed her car door shut, and hurried out of earshot of the garage.

"Why someone needs to use that kind of language is beyond me," she muttered as she entered the park, which was already alive with vendors, visitors, musicians, and what Maggie considered much too much life at this early hour.

Still, even though she did not care for being in crowds, Maggie found herself enjoying the sights and smells and sounds of the outdoor market. The colors of silk scarves, handmade quilts, and the paintings of local artists made Maggie feel she was in a completely different place and nowhere near Fair Haven. It was fun to pretend she was in an open marketplace somewhere like Calabria, Italy, where people haggled and negotiated the prices of their wares and the food was delicious because it was homemade from a recipe passed down from generation to generation. As she came up on the first vendor cooking over a steaming grill, she saw traditional hotdogs and hamburgers.

So, it isn't some exotic Italian cuisine. It still smells fantastic, Maggie thought. How her sister could walk past this and not want a burger with everything and opt for tofu and bean sprouts instead was beyond her. The thought brought her back to the small town of Fair Haven and the death of Echo Manns. As if by divine intervention, Maggie suddenly spied two of the people who had been in the bookstore the previous day. They were Leather-Bicep-Strap-Man and Mr. Birkenstocks.

Quickly, Maggie scanned the area for Grisham. He gave her the heebie-jeebies. There was something about his gaze and the words he said to her that rubbed her the wrong way. She didn't see him, but what she did see made her angry.

"Can you explain to me why this one is this price and this one is more? They look the same. How did you come to this price?" Mr. Birkenstock asked the young girl, who was standing alone at a long table with crystal doodads, suncatchers, and jewelry. While Mr. Birkenstock was getting testy, Mr. Leather-Bicep-Strap was slipping several crystal items into his pockets.

"Hey!" Maggie shouted and pointed. "Hey! I see what you're doing!" All heads turned in her direction, and for a second she felt like a hot, blinding spotlight had just found her. But when she saw the glare from the two GSA members, she felt emboldened.

"What?" The young girl looked from Maggie to the two men then quickly scanned her inventory. In a matter of seconds, the girl realized that a few small items were missing.

"I saw you put something in your pocket!" Maggie called as she quickly approached but didn't get too close. Something made her think they might put a spell on her if she did. By now, a crowd had stopped to watch.

"What are you talking about? Mind your own business," Mr. Birkenstock snapped.

"Your friend just put something from her table in his pocket." Maggie pointed at the arm-banded man.

"She's crazy. Come on, let's go," Mr. Birkenstock replied as he looked at his companion and rolled his eyes. However, it wasn't that easy. A large man in a T-shirt and leather vest walked up to the duo, and although he didn't put a hand on them, he had something to say.

"If you have anything in your pockets from my booth, I'm giving you the chance now to put it back," he said. His bald head shined, and his eyes looked like perfect chocolate-colored marbles beneath thick bushy eyebrows.

"Look, she's just making things up," Mr. Birkenstock continued, but his friend was looking skittish as the owner of the booth took half a step closer.

"There are three sets missing, Pop-Pop." The girl behind the booth pointed at a section of her table where the arm-banded man had been standing just a few minutes ago.

Maggie was not only shocked the big brute was the creator of such elegant and dainty crystal pieces but also that such a cute and delicate young lady called him Pop-Pop.

"They are part of a group! I nearly broke the arm of one of their gang the other day when he tried to swipe my till! Long hair and green eyes! He's smart enough not to come back!" A man in bib overalls emerged from the smoke of his grill, which Maggie had just passed, and pointed a long fork in their direction. "None of you will make it out of Fair Haven, I'll promise you that!" he shouted.

Maggie made a mental note of the man's business. *Lou's Better Beef.* He had to be Lou.

When Maggie turned back, she saw Pop-Pop was not happy.

"If you boys will just return what you took, I'll let this go. I don't want to involve the police if I don't have to. But I will, and you can bet there will be an altercation before they arrive. A bruised ego heals quickly. A bruised face… not so much."

"Yeah! Just ask your friend! I'm sure you noticed he wasn't quite himself!" Lou barked.

The leather-bicep-strap-man nervously reached into his pocket just as Mr. Birkenstock was shaking his head as if there was nothing to see here. Both men blushed crimson as Leather-Bicep-Strap-Man slyly slipped the merchandise from his pocket and onto the table.

"I had stuff stolen from my table yesterday by a couple of your folks. You think you can come to a small town and take advantage, and we won't do anything? I'll politely ask you two gentlemen to leave now," the brute said, his eyes staring intently into the eyes of the two GSA members.

Mr. Birkenstock stomped off in a huff like a teenager being denied the car on Friday night. To his credit, his partner extended his hand to the bald man and offered a sincere apology that the man accepted. The bald man whispered a couple of things Maggie couldn't hear before he let go of the other man's hand. Judging by the look on Leather-Bicep-Strap-Man's face, whatever words were exchanged danced on the verge of a threat.

Maggie watched the two GSA members slink off. Mr. Birkenstock was not happy and glared at her before pulling his partner along by his leather-strapped bicep.

"Thank you, miss," Pop-Pop said to Maggie, making her blush too.

She gave an awkward smile before pushing her glasses up on her nose. Without wanting to make it look like she was going to chase the perpetrators,

Maggie looked at the lovely crystal designs and then at the young girl. She smiled, showing braces Maggie hadn't noticed before. Those two jerks were trying to lift from a girl who probably hadn't even finished high school, which made her wonder if they would have tried to recruit her too. Would they whisper nonsense to her that only a young, starry-eyed youth would understand, and would that convince to her to leave her Pop-Pop, who obviously loved her? Would they have gotten her to disappear from her family like they did with Angel?

With the excitement over and resulting in nothing more than a couple words and no punches exchanged, the crowd quickly dispersed. When Maggie looked around, she saw quite a few people looking approvingly at her.

She wove through the crowd until she spotted the two GSA members. They were hurrying along, not bothering to stop at any of the other booths. The urge to steal from anyone else had fizzled with being caught and humiliated in front of the fine folks of Fair Haven.

"I can't believe you, Mike," Mr. Birkenstock scolded.

"What is your problem? Better to just let it go, Neal. There are other things we can do." Maggie was close enough to hear their bickering and thought they sounded like they'd been through this more than once. They were behaving like children if she had to be honest. Neal's bad influence had yet to totally corrupt Mike, who looked to be only halfway interested in what Neal was saying. Maggie wouldn't want to listen to Neal either.

She kept her distance as she followed and was surprised when they emerged from the park and made their way to the Copper Tower Hotel, the fanciest hotel in Fair Haven. These guys were stealing from the locals yet somehow finagled rooms at the Copper Tower? That didn't make any sense to Maggie.

Their bickering continued all the way across the street and through the revolving doors leading to the lobby. Maggie followed. As soon as she entered the hotel, she quickly slipped behind a large potted plant and watched as Neal and Mike went to the desk of the concierge. By the look on his face, Maggie gathered he'd dealt with the duo before now. His slight eyeroll and the way his chest deflated when they approached reminded Maggie of how she often felt when people approached her with questions at the bookstore.

The Copper Tower Hotel boasted old-time

charm with modern conveniences. It had only twenty-five rooms, but from the word around town was that each one was beautiful.

As Maggie sat on one of the vintage-looking loveseats, she never let Neal and Mike out of the corner of her eye. On the walls hung paintings of fox hunts and stoic patrons in golden frames. Large, intricately designed vases decorated the lobby, and richly colored Persian rugs beneath the furniture. The people behind the front desk wore crisp black blazers with striking white shirts beneath. The bell-hops were equally starched as they bustled back and forth with racks of luggage coming in and out of the service doors. Over strategically placed speakers, old-time singers could be heard softly singing songs reminiscing about the past. This hotel was the kind of place Maggie could easily see Sam Spade stopping in to get out of the rain and shake off his fedora or Daisy Buchanan hoping to purr at Gatsby once more before her husband arrived.

But none of literature's greatest characters were loitering around. The guests were just regular tourists and families who had decided on Fair Haven for the weekend and a little down-home hospitality in the fanciest digs in town.

Maggie carefully inched her way toward the

concierge's desk with her back to the two men and stooped low to peruse a display of local attractions. Once again, she heard Neal doing all the double-talking. Their discussion had something to do with housekeeping and an extra key and that room service had stopped earlier than noted on the in-room menu. They didn't have enough towels or toiletries.

"…but, sir, I can't issue a key for a room you are not staying in. None of the associates at the hotel can," the concierge said.

"We are all together. Surely your manager had informed you that we were special guests of the hotel. Mr. Grisham is a very important man. You'd do well to speak with him. But at the moment, I need to get into his room and…"

Maggie decided Neal was very needy. He was also a jerk and would not let up on the concierge one bit. Over and over, he made him repeat the rule that keys could not just be thrown around willy-nilly no matter who was staying at the hotel or making the request.

"That's the man!" someone said suddenly in a loud, booming voice from the revolving door. It was Lou from Lou's Better Beef. A vein bulged from the middle of his head, and his eyebrows were pulled down so far over his eyes they cast them in a dark, menacing shadow. There was another man behind him who at first Maggie thought was a policeman, but upon closer inspection of his uniform, she realized he was nothing more than one of the park maintenance guys.

Neal stared, his mouth hanging open. Mike made his way to the stairs.

"You watch your wallets and purses!" Lou shouted. "That man is a thief! He tried to steal my till! I'm just an honest man trying to make a living! Now he tried to steal from a young lady selling her jewelry! We all saw it! I'm warning you now! You'll get worse than that friend of yours if I see you around the grounds again!"

Neal turned his attention back to the concierge, who was grateful for the diversion. The hotel security guard quickly rushed over to Lou and, with his hands raised, asked Lou to leave the hotel.

"If you don't have a room here, sir, I have to ask you to leave," the guard said calmly.

"I'll be watching you! Don't think you can get away with stealing around here! You or your friends!" Lou shouted.

"Sir, please. I need you to leave the premises," the guard said, continuing to maintain his cool.

"I'm going. I'm going. You're lucky this guard is here, you no-good piece of trash! Or you'd learn a lesson like your friend did!" Lou shouted at Neal before he and the park maintenance man left.

Maggie looked at Neal again, who was busy looking down, his face completely flushed. Mike shook his head and proceeded to walk up the stairs. Without waiting, Maggie followed. At the second landing, Mike took a left, so Maggie went to the right and pressed herself flat against the first door. If the members of the SGA weren't looking for her, she didn't think they'd see her hiding there. Just as she was about to peek and see where Mike had gone, Neal came stomping up the stairs and also went to the left.

"What the heck, Mike?" he hissed.

"This is a mess, Neal. I think we should abandon this one. What is it about this girl that Grisham is so determined to bring her back for? We've had a couple of deserters before her, and he never acted like this. You aren't telling me everything," Mike argued.

"Just get in the room," Neal barked, shoving Mike. Still mumbling, they went into a room at the end of the hallway. Maggie emerged from her hiding place and quickly hurried to the closed door.

With a quick glance up and down the hallway, she pressed her ear to the door and held her breath.

"It isn't the girl. It's Echo. He's worth a lot of money," Earl said.

"So why are we chasing down Angel? I know she's hot but…"

"Because Grisham says so. Now, we need to let things calm down because of you and…"

"Because of me? You're the one who…"

"Enough!"

Even Maggie jumped back from the door when Neal shouted. Suddenly, she heard the ding of the elevator just a few feet away. Holding her chin high, she walked away from the door as if strolling down the hallway was as normal as getting off the elevator. The sound of wheels catching on the lip of the carpet and the jiggling of bottles gave away the identity of the person approaching. When Maggie looked over her shoulder, sure enough, she saw the housekeeper. The smell of bleach and lemony cleaning materials quickly filled the hallway.

The housekeeper smiled briefly at Maggie as if she really had something else on her mind. "Do you want housekeeping?" the woman asked politely.

Maggie realized she was standing in front of room 210 as if she was about to go inside.

"Oh, yes. But I can't find my key. I forgot my map of Fair Haven in there." She rolled her eyes and guffawed like a clumsy tourist while patting every pocket and looking down at her shoes as if the key or map might be there.

"I've got it," the housekeeper said with a slight hint of annoyance in her voice. As soon as she unlocked the door to 210, the door to room 214, where Neal and Mike were staying, flew open. They continued their argument but stopped as soon as they saw a lone woman in the hallway. Maggie pressed herself against the door of room 210 and listened.

"Excuse me, ma'am." Neal once again *had* to hassle someone in passing.

"Yes, sir," the housekeeper replied politely.

"If you could leave us a couple of extra towels and blankets, that would be wonderful. We had requested them last night, but they never arrived," Neal said and clicked his tongue while tilting his head to the right.

As she listened, Maggie wondered how many people were sleeping in that room at once.

"Yes, I'll make sure to leave some extra towels and have a blanket sent up," the housekeeper said.

She fumbled around with her cleaning bottles and tucked a roll of toilet paper under her arm.

"Thank you. All the blessing of love and light on you and yours," Neal replied before he and Mike resumed their bickering as they slipped into the elevator.

Maggie shook her head but still let out a long sigh of relief. Then she hitched her breath in the back of her throat. She had an idea.

Chapter 9

As she heard the housekeeper shuffle her way, Maggie grabbed the hotel pamphlet from the desk of room 210, hoping the occupants wouldn't need it. With a spring in her step, she bopped out of room 210 like she owned it and pulled the door closed behind her with a thick thud and a click of the lock. After thanking the housekeeper for her kind help, Maggie walked to the stairs. Once around the corner, she waited for the woman to go into room 214. If it was laid out anything like room 210, Maggie could easily slip inside and hide in the closet next to the door until the housekeeper left. Her heart pounded in her ears as she waited and tried to figure out a reason not to try this.

It was for Angel. If they thought she had anything to do with Echo's death, something in that room might help prove her sister was innocent. There was no way she could leave a single stone unturned, no matter how big it was.

Finally, Maggie heard the cleaning lady move her cart. When she peeked around the corner, she saw her at room 214. The woman stepped in, using her cart to hold the door open. With her arms full of towels, she entered the room. Maggie hurried to the door and listened. The housekeeper was humming a tune Maggie didn't recognize, but it sounded like she was deep inside the room. Maggie took a deep breath and held it. With every muscle rigid and stiff, she stepped into the doorway. No housekeeper in sight. Although her face was calm, her eyes darted around wildly. The closet was right there and, as luck would have it, slightly open. Maggie slipped her delicate fingers along the edge and slowly slid it open farther to slip inside. Once there, Maggie pushed herself to the farthest corner like a spider and waited. The cleaning lady did a thorough job of cleaning the bathroom and making the beds. But then something made her talk out loud.

"Oh, now, this is just too much. What is wrong

with people? I'll never know. Why do they feel the need to leave these kinds of things around? Just put the dirty plates outside the door," she said with a huff as Maggie heard the rattling of plates and silverware.

Neal and Mike must have ordered room service and left the plates somewhere the housekeeper didn't like.

Maggie's neck started to ache as she tilted her head to the right to fit under the shelf that ran the length of the closet. The smell of lemon cleaner that had just a few minutes before been rather pleasant was now becoming too much. The scent tickled the inside of Maggie's nostrils, threatening to force out a sneeze that would most definitely give away her position. She reached up, pinched her nose shut, and breathed through her mouth.

Just then, the housekeeper, quiet as a church mouse as she padded around the room, slid open the other closet door, flooding the small space in light that just narrowly reached Maggie's hiding place. The housekeeper had obviously done this a million times, and the thought of looking inside the closet for a stranger or a monster that might be lurking there had not crossed her mind. Still, Maggie squeezed her eyes shut as if doing so might keep her presence a secret. It worked. The house-keeper took a hanger and a few seconds later reached back inside the closet to hang up a denim jacket. Before Maggie could exhale, the house-keeper slid the doors to the closet shut. Maggie was safe for the time being. After listening to the house-keeper sing, hum, and talk to herself Maggie finally heard the door to the room slam and the automatic lock slip into place.

Even though she was sure she was alone, Maggie waited and listened a few seconds more. There was no movement of any kind in the room. Tenderly, she slipped her fingers along the edge of the door and pushed it open. The room smelled fresh and lemony. The light from the parted curtains was bright and made her blink after being in the dark closet. She put her hand to her neck and stretched the kinks out. Maggie had been bent unnaturally to the right for longer than she should have.

The room looked like any other hotel room. Room 210 looked just like this one. Except for two old duffle bags, one on the bed and another on a chair, there was hardly any difference.

"What are you even looking for?" Maggie asked. She hurried to the first duffle bag and looked through it. Sadly, it was harmless enough, with nothing but T-shirts and socks and toiletries in it. The other duffle bag was almost identical but for a pair of flip-flops tucked at the bottom.

The thought that maybe there was nothing more to these guys than exactly what they were crossed Maggie's mind. Maybe they were just petty thieves who stole here and there to get by in the real world, but once they were back on their compound, they made a living selling their organic vegetables and homemade soap.

Nothing in particula drew her attention to the desk. There were always pamphlets, paper menus, and Do Not Disturb signs laying around. But as Maggie leaned over to take a closer look, she was shocked to see a spreadsheet consisting of a couple of pages stapled together with her sister's name on the top line.

"What is this?"

She read the document. There was Angel's full name, birthday, height, weight, like they'd collected her information from her driver's license. The document also listed Maggie's name and address along with her home address and the Bookish Café's address. The spreadsheet went on to list many other things. Personal things. Things that only Angel and only her closest friends would know, like her cycle and the scar she had on her thigh from when she'd trespassed on a neighbor's property and caught herself on the barbed wire. Maggie saw vague details about their father, but that didn't matter. The document did describe Maggie's relationship with Angel as *strained*. Whatever was going on between her and her sister was no one's business.

"Our relationship isn't strained. It's no different from any other relationship between siblings. We are two very different people, that's all," she insisted, scanning the descriptions of the other people on the list. They all had similar notes added. From the looks of it, all the people the GSA were searching for had "strained" relationships. There was a pattern. Maggie couldn't help but think they targeted certain people who they could say had strained relationships and use that to manipulate their members. That was nothing any other cult hadn't done before. But it didn't take a genius to know that the possibility of another Jonestown lay just inches away from this kind of fanaticism.

Maggie didn't recognize any of the other names, but it looked like they were searching for these people, just as they were Angel. There was a total of fourteen names with similar descriptions. What stood out next to Angel's name was a red X.

"What does that mean? That they found her? Or that they are going to...get rid of her? Take her back?"

Maggie pursed her lips. Clearly, the Greater Society of Atonement had some extensive ways of collecting information on their members and using it to their advantage. As Maggie looked over the desk, she saw another interesting piece of information—a receipt for a pawn shop. But not just any pawn shop. Hawes Pawn Shop. But just as she was about to voice her disdain, she heard voices outside the door and the click of the key in the lock.

Chapter 10

Without enough time to return to the closet, Maggie scanned the room and hid in the only place she could get to quickly enough. She held her breath and braced herself against the wall with the curtain pulled over her. It was a painful balancing act on the tips of her toes so they wouldn't peek out from beneath the hem of the heavy fabric. But if anyone wanted to let in more light, they would discover more than the view of town.

"We need the money," Neal said from the other side.

"So why not just unload it at the same place?" Mike asked. Today was not his day, since once again Neal snapped at him.

"We can't go to the same pawn shop so soon after just stopping there. That will make him suspicious, for sure. The last thing we need is for there to be a bunch of eyes looking at us. After your stunt today, I'm surprised we haven't been visited by the local sheriff."

Maggie didn't like Neal. He was a bully and a manipulator, and she was sure had they not been in a cult, brainwashed into following orders, Mike might have had enough sense to tell Neal to go take a flying leap.

"That wasn't my fault. It was that girl. Angel's sister," Mike said. Maggie changed her opinion of him immediately. He deserved every bossy comment he got.

"Yeah, she's going to be trouble. But Grisham has a plan to get Angel back, and with Angel we'll have Echo. Keeping Echo happy is the main goal. If we ruffle a couple of feathers, that's what happens."

"What does Grisham plan to do about it?"

Maggie pushed away the pain in her toes and tried to listen. Her heels felt burned into her calves. Any move to adjust her weight or attempt to get comfortable would risk her giving away her position. She began to sweat.

"I'm not sure. But it will all work out," Mike said. Maggie hearda zipper and then someone shaking a pill bottle. "I have something else we can sell if things get tough."

"Did Grisham approve that?" Mike had the courage to ask.

"I'll talk to him about it when we see him." Neal let out a long deep breath. "It wouldn't be the first time. Believe me, we only do it in an emergency. This is an emergency."

"Yeah, I guess so. Is he meeting us here when he's done talking with the guy at the bookstore?" Mike asked. Maggie felt her heart race. What were they planning to do with Joshua? The Bookish Café was the only bookstore in town. If they thought they could work him over into giving up information on her or Angel, they would have much more trouble than they anticipated. Once Maggie got the feeling back in her toes and calves, she would be ready to stand toe-to-toe with anyone to protect her sister.

Especially since now she knew they weren't really interested in her. They wanted Echo, and he was missing in action. Maybe he'd seen through their plan, and Grisham had something to do with him falling at the Hickory Creek Bridge. Maybe he was pretending to be concerned so no one would look for him.

Maggie grimaced as a sharp pain shot up her leg. She wished that Mike and Neal would get what they came for and leave so she could at least hide in the closet again if she had to. This was by far one of her worst ideas. She pressed her palms against the wall, finding it a rough chalky stucco that offered nothing but its cold texture in return.

"No. Didn't he say we were to meet him here around five?" Maggie's heart jumped when she heard Mike say that. No way would she be able to stay put for over three hours while these numbskulls pretended to be some kind of New Agers when they were really nothing more than criminals in hemp clothing. The pain in her legs was travelling up to her knees and thighs. Her lower back felt like it was being compressed down by her upper back, and her hands were sweating terribly.

"No. We're supposed to meet him in the park," Neal replied.

"Do you think that's a good idea? I mean, with all the trouble that was caused today," Mike said sheepishly.

"We'll stay away from that part of the park. It

won't be hard for Grisham to find us. Come on, let's get going."

"Don't you think we could stay here for an hour or so?" Mike asked. Maggie hadn't taken a full breath since she took up her hiding place, and now her breath caught in her throat.

She'd be crippled for sure if she stayed there much longer.

"No. We need to continue our work. There are a lot of lost people out there. Just because we are looking for someone doesn't mean we can let our real purpose sit on the sidelines," Neal said. "We'll be rewarded. And if there is any way to get back into the family's good graces, it is to get more recruits."

There was no mistaking the tone of Neal's voice that he expected Mike to rustle up some naïve suckers who might be willing to join their group. What kind of people would be interested in what they had to say? What did the group promise that sounded so great? And if Echo had all this money, why did he feel the need to leave his family to beg and steal for necessities with this group?

"Yeah. I guess you are right," Mike conceded. He sounded like a boy who was desperately trying to get the approval of the adults around him by doing what he really didn't want to do. "Neal, I'm sorry I made such a scene today."

Maggie could hardly believe her ears. Did they know she was there? Were they saying all this to shock her into revealing herself? How could Mike apologize for doing the right thing after getting caught doing the wrong thing? He got busted and made it right by shaking Pop-Pop's hand, and now he was sorry for that? What kind of backwards group was this?

"It's all right, Mike. We all make mistakes. That's how you learn. Next time you'll do things exactly the way you are supposed to, and you'll see that those who follow directions are rewarded by the universe," Neal blathered.

Maggie thought he sounded like a creepy camp counselor who wanted to hide that he allowed the kids to drink and smoke.

"So, what should we do with this stuff?" Mike asked.

"Leave it here. No one will be in the room. We can make sure we pawn it all tomorrow. If we have to use the van to go to another pawn shop, I'm sure Grisham will allow it," Mike said before they fussed around the room for a few minutes. To Maggie, whose thighs were burning and whose toes were slowly starting to lose all feeling except for millions of tiny pins and needles, the two GSA members couldn't move fast enough. Once the door slammed shut, she eased herself down onto her flat feet and let out a groan of relief. Her toes instantly peeked out from beneath the curtains. She let out a breath that she felt she'd been holding for hours and rubbed her thighs, hoping to get the feeling back in them.

On the desk where she'd found the receipt to Hawes Pawn Shop were a thin gold chain, an antique pocket watch, and a gold ring with an pearl in it. Without hesitating, she scooped them up in her hand and hobbled to the door, her toes, ankles, and thighs still screaming in relief. She didn't care who was on the other side of the door. Whether it was Neal and Mike or the housekeeper, Maggie was getting out of there. Her nerves were shot, and she could only imagine what damage she'd done to her feet by holding that position for so long.

She was on her toes for a total of only about ten minutes. A ballet dancer did an hour-long performance or longer on her toes. But as Maggie would happily tell anyone, she was not a dancer, and her rubber-soled Mary Janes were not the kind of shoes one should use to balance on their toes.

The hallway was empty except for the house-keeping cart when Maggie opened the door and stepped out. She stuffed the jewelry into her pocket. But she didn't have the receipt to Hawes Pawn Shop. If she were to confront Neal on what the GSA members were doing pawning stolen goods and why was he accepting them when he knew they were stolen, she needed that receipt. The thought came to her just as the door to room 214 slipped softly shut, the lock clicking into place like someone clucking their tongue in disappointment. Maggie's shoulders slumped as she felt deflated.

Chapter 11

All she wanted was to get out of the Copper Tower Hotel and never return, but the hotel seemed to have different ideas. It wanted to keep her here. That theme sounded familiar. Maggie read it in a book somewhere, and the recollection sent shivers up her spine.

"One of Dante's rings of hell was never being able to leave the Copper Tower Hotel. Hmm... it rhymes," she muttered as the housekeeper emerged down the hall to retrieve some fresh towels and retreat into the room. Just then, the elevator dinged, and another woman in housekeeping attire hustled past Maggie without so much as a "hello" or "get out of my way."

There was a snippy exchange inside the hotel room before the other housekeeper Maggie had spoken to emerged and grumbled away in the direction of the stairs.

"Excuse me." Maggie wrinkled her nose and gingerly rapped on the open door to room 212. The housekeeper who had slipped in turned around quickly. She was a plump woman with a couple of chins and a serious look about her. She inspected Maggie, and Maggie was sure that like a CCT might capture every detail of how she looked, so did this housekeeper.

"Yes?" the woman replied.

"My boyfriend left a receipt he needs in room 214. He's lost our keys and is getting a new one from the front desk. Can you let me in the room to get it?" Maggie said, cringing slightly at the idea of Neal being anyone's boyfriend, let alone hers. Even in make-believe, it was a gross proposal.

"I didn't clean room 214," the housekeeper replied without any emotion as her eyes scanned the room, but she remained stationary. "The other maid did."

"Do you mind if I take a quick look? He's waiting for me downstairs," Maggie said, surprised at how easily she was able to conjure up this fake emergency.

"Why doesn't he come and look himself?" the housekeeper replied.

"Oh, you know how men are," Maggie said with a titter as she stayed at the threshold of the door. With her nose wrinkled, she hoped she looked innocent because she felt her lie was as big as a billboard over her head.

"We aren't supposed to do that," this housekeeper replied with the same kind of firmness as the previous woman.

"Please? I will be in and out. I swear. I know exactly where it is. It's on the nightstand. In fact, I don't even have to go in the room. You could, and then no one would be breaking the rules. See?" Maggie smiled awkwardly.

This housekeeper let out an annoyed sigh, which made Maggie wonder just how many requests like this housekeepers got on a daily basis. She would have assumed almost none, since the chances of anyone else trying to clear their sister of a murder was pretty slim. But by the reactions of these employees, it appeared they were inconvenienced frequently.

"I've got a schedule to keep. If I fall behind

now, I'll be behind for the rest of my shift," the woman said and went back to her work.

"I wouldn't have asked if it wasn't really important," Maggie said, her voice cracking. She sniffled and gave her best pathetic expression. In her mind, she looked like a sad bulldog unable to play outside because of the rain. In reality, she looked constipated.

The housekeeper tossed the towels on the counter in the bathroom, shaking her head. "I'll go in and get it. You stay right here."

"Yes, ma'am. Thank you," Maggie replied. But under three seconds later, she realized she'd made a mistake. The housekeeper walked over to the nightstand but saw no receipt there. What was Maggie thinking? It was on the desk, plain and simple for everyone to see. She could see it from the door.

"There is no receipt here," the housekeeper snapped and put her hand on her hip.

Quickly, Maggie entered the room and pointed at the desk. "It's here. I guess…"

"You aren't supposed to be in this room!" the housekeeper shouted, making Maggie freeze.

"I'm just trying to help and…"

"*You* said it was on the nightstand, and it wasn't. There isn't anything on the nightstand." The housekeeper looked Maggie up and down as if she might be smuggling the comforter or a lamp under her shirt.

"I meant the desk, and if you'd just…" Maggie pointed at the desk and took a few steps forward. She saw the ticket she was looking for. It was just sitting there. What value was a receipt? There was no money there. This was a flimsy piece of paper that had no value to anyone but her.

The housekeeper shook her head and looked down to pull something from her pocket. As she did, Maggie advanced, stretched, and put her hand over the receipt. Quickly she balled it up as the housekeeper let out a long, annoyed sigh and pulled out her walkie-talkie.

"Clairice?" she said into the small black box.

"Yes, Rhonda," a staticky voice replied over the radio.

"I'm in 214, and there is a lady here who wants to look for something. She says the man whose room this is is in the lobby. Anyone down there by the name of Neal?" Rhonda asked.

"I'll just go and tell Neal he has to look himself," Maggie replied, tucking her hand holding the receipt behind her back as she backed up toward the door.

"There isn't anyone in the lobby, Rhonda," Clairice replied. "Was she in the hallway before?"

Maggie's heart was set to burst out of her chest. She'd already snuck into the room before, and Clairice's voice sounded awfully familiar. If she was the same person Maggie had spoken to before, it would be a matter of minutes until Officer Gary Brookes got there, shaking his head and leading her out of the hotel in handcuffs for robbing a hotel room. She wasn't concerned with the robbery part. It was having Gary as the arresting officer. She'd never live it down.

"Clairice, maybe you should come up here and talk to *this person*," Rhonda said, pinching her lips together as she stared intently at Maggie.

"There really is no need," Maggie said.

"Stay right there, young lady." Rhonda pointed an accusatory finger at Maggie.

Maggie's heart jumped and prompted her feet into action. Before she could call up Clairice on the radio, Maggie bolted for the door and down the hallway. Part of her thought maybe she should slow down and walk calmly and carefully out of the hotel as if she were just a guest taking a casual stroll. But another part of her said to keep running. As room 214 got farther and farther behind her, she was sure she heard Rhonda giving a detailed description of her clothes, hair and face. She had her height and weight down within one number, and Maggie was sure she also heard Clairice calling the police simultaneously. With total disregard for her own safety, Maggie jumped from the second step to the landing and with a thud to the first floor. Then she leapt with the most graceful technique she could muster to the lobby level and pushed herself off the edge of a table, spinning in a complete circle before making her getaway out the revolving door.

In her mind, and if she was to retell the caper to anyone, she was as nimble as a gazelle leaping over a bubbling brook and landing firmly before pivoting her body with perfect timing to make a clean, almost seamless escape. In reality, the concierge and Clairice were the only ones who witnessed Maggie's performance of staggering and bumbling her way down the stairs like a drunken sailor and having a mini-spasm as she struggled to push the revolving door faster than it could move.

Once her feet hit the sidewalk, Maggie quickly made her way to the park where she slipped into the meandering crowd and caught her breath. After watching over her shoulder for a few minutes, she was sure she hadn't been followed. Maggie had successfully given her pursuers the slip. With pride, she straightened her back and squared her shoulders as she unfolded the crumpled receipt in her hand.

"Hawes Pawn Shop," she muttered. Roger Hawes had a way of leaving a bad taste in Maggie's mouth. He'd been after Mr. Whitfield to sell the bookstore to him for years. He'd come in every couple of months to talk about how bad the book business was and how Mr. Whitfield better get out before he got buried.

"In order to break even, you'd have to demolish the whole building," Roger would say, then click his tongue and shake his head. "I'm making you a good offer."

That was a joke in itself. Roger Hawes never made a good offer to anyone. He knew how much the building was worth just like he knew how much every piece of merchandise was worth in each one of the display cases at his pawn shops.

"We don't want to sell," Mr. Whitfield would reply lazily as he rocked in his chair behind his desk. Maggie never knew whether it was Roger's imbecilic comments or her facial expressions that made him smirk more.

"Who is *we*?" Roger would ask every single time.

"Miss Bell and me," he'd reply, and every time Roger would scoff and roll his eyes. Maggie was sure that he thought she was to blame for Mr. Whitfield never handing over the deed. Something about Hawes that always made Maggie believe he thought the seediest things about every person he ever encountered. Now she was going to speak to him on his turf.

Hawes Pawn Shop was not far from Patrick Cusic's garage. The whole ordeal made Maggie crinkle her face. It seemed like all the unsavory people were located in the same part of town. As she looked at the receipt, she wondered how the Greater Society of Atonement, a group of people who gave up all their material goods, were able to pawn an eighteen-inch gold chain, a diamond tennis bracelet, and an amethyst ring.

Maggie drove to the pawn shop. She squeezed her Dodge Neon in between an old Cadillac that was as big as a boat and a Harley-Davidson motorcycle. Once she was parked, she took a deep breath and collected herself. The last thing she wanted was a replay of the panic-mode she'd put on full display at the hotel.

A few things tickled at the back of her mind. First and foremost was where the Great Society of Atonement got those items from. She wanted to see them. She had a gut feeling that they were not the typical style of accessories the Greater Society of Atonement members would wear. There probably wasn't much money in hocking leather arm straps.

Chapter 12

After her harrowing experience at the Copper Tower Hotel, Maggie gulped down the fresh air as she hustled down the sidewalk like she'd been underwater for hours. With one careful look over her shoulder she was confident that the housekeeping staff was *not* in pursuit.

Her stomach growled. The knowledge that she couldn't remember the last time she'd eaten had seized her. She remembered a sandwich somewhere, maybe a Pop-Tart or a can of soup. This was bad. It was all Angel's fault. She had Maggie so nervous and upset she was forgetting the basic necessities required to remain upright.

This was what always happened. Angel went

and took up a new hobby or some man who was anything but normal, and everyone else had to walk behind her while she maneuvered the tightrope, waiting to catch her if she fell. Maggie recalled her first night in Mrs. Peacock's house when she had no real furniture and nothing more than a can of sardines and crackers until she got to the store. No one asked if she was all right. Not a soul offered to give her a leg up to make things easier.

"Why would they, Mags?" she asked. "You'd never do the crazy things she does."

She rubbed her stomach again and thought that she wanted something different to eat. At first, she considered going to one of the vendors in the park. The whole place smelled good, and she thought of Lou's Better Beef but then reconsidered it. The last thing she wanted was to confront the man who confronted the GSA members. But she did wonder what he meant when he spoke about making an example of one of their members.

"He's just a guy who was mad over being robbed," Maggie muttered. "That would make any man mad, especially a guy just trying to sell his product."

But if he did something to Echo, then that would clear any doubt that might be cast on Angel.

"Why do you even care? Would Angel go through all this for you?" Maggie's mumbles made several passersby look at her with raised eyebrows. She didn't care.

As she contemplated her own words, her shoulders slumped. In truth, if Angel thought Maggie was in trouble, she would help. Maggie knew she would. And if she couldn't do it herself, she'd find someone else who could. With renewed confidence in the task at hand, Maggie decided that she needed to eat first and would then go talk to Lou's Better Beef. Just as an idea for food popped in her head, she heard someone calling her name.

"Maggie."

She turned and saw Joyce from the bank waving to her. Maggie's face instantly crinkled, as she thought first that something was wrong with the last deposit she made and then that Joyce had to be the one to inform her about it.

Maggie and Joyce had a strange history. It was nonexistent until Joshua Whitfield came to town. Then, because he was a handsome single man, half the single women of Fair Haven, including Joyce, took an interest in him. However, Joyce was the most blatant in her attempt to gain the bachelor's attention by any means necessary, including trying to grill Maggie about his schedule and habits.

"Hey, Maggie. How are you?" Joyce's forced smile was almost as crooked as Maggie's.

"Fine. Is there something wrong with the account?" Maggie asked without the slightest bit of emotion in her voice.

"Oh, no. No, not at all. I'm just saying hello," Joyce replied. "I saw your window at the bookstore. Joshua did an amazing job."

Maggie shook her shoulders, as though a shiver ran up her spine. "I did the window. I do all the window displays. Everybody knows that. Joshua doesn't know how to decorate a display window. He barely knows how to dress himself or make a bed or even get a close shave," Maggie muttered mostly under her breath like a person answering voices only she heard.

"Oh." Joyce folded her arms over her chest wrinkling her blouse and bunching up the sleeves of her blazer. She was obviously coming from the bank, since this was her usual bank attire.

"Okay, now that we've cleared that up," Maggie mumbled and put her head down to walk away just as Joyce stepped in her way.

"Will Joshua be at the fireworks display?" Joyce asked.

"I don't know," Maggie replied.

"Has he mentioned anything about it? The whole town is going to be there. I was just wondering if he was going."

"Why don't you ask him? I'm not his secretary."

"You're the one who is always with him. Well, you were. I've seen him walking with your sister a lot. What's that all about?"

There was the real issue. Joyce had seen Joshua and Angel together, and it got her dander up. If anyone else were bringing up Joshua and her sister, maybe Maggie would have felt that twist of jealousy in her gut. After all, Maggie was no different from many of the ladies in town who thought he was handsome and smart and funny and all the things that made a good boyfriend. But this was an outsider speaking with a negative tone about her half sister.

"How do you know it's my sister?" Maggie asked.

"It's all over town that Maggie Bell's sister is here. She's been seen at the park and at all the events. Last night's bonfire and the beanbag toss competition earlier in the afternoon. She's been chatting with just about everyone. It doesn't take long for word to spread in this town." Joyce rocked from side to side as if she was getting ready to sprint away. Maggie looked down at her shoes. They were red slip-ons that were rather cute if you could get past that they had to be a size ten or bigger. Maggie thought red was not the color she should be wearing on her feet. You'd want to draw attention away from those clodhoppers.

"What my sister does and with who is really no one else's business," Maggie said. "But when I see her at home tonight, I'll tell her you are looking for her and have some questions. I'm sure she'd be happy to discuss her social life with you," Maggie tried to push her way past Joyce, but the woman, who towered over Maggie by at least five inches, blocked her path.

"There is no reason to get snippy with me, Margaret," Joyce said.

Maggie looked at her and rubbed her stomach, which started to gurgle. If she didn't get some food quickly, she was sure she was going to pass out. The last person she'd want picking her up off the sidewalk was Joyce from the bank. All right, that might have been completely dramatic and not nearly close to the truth. But Maggie was feeling her skin start to itch as she tried to inch her way past Joyce, not caring if she came across as rude or insensitive.

"I'm not being snippy. This is how I always act," she replied and pushed her glasses up as she slid past the woman. But Maggie couldn't help herself and continued to mutter. "Especially around people like you. Joshua isn't interested, and neither are the other men in town. It doesn't have anything to do with my sister."

"What did you just say?" Joyce snapped.

"Nothing. Bye, Joyce." Maggie shook her head like she'd been off in a daydream.

"You're so weird," Joyce hissed and grimaced before plodding away, her size-ten feet slapping against the sidewalk.

Maggie had a bitter taste in her mouth. That was not uncommon when she had to deal with people. Especially people she didn't like, such as Joyce. As much as she didn't want to admit it, Maggie wondered if Joshua had been spending time with Angel because he was interested in her. He didn't mention anything about it to Maggie. She didn't see him walking around the café and bookstore in a lovestruck daze or asking questions about Angel like what her favorite flower was or if she enjoyed chocolate candies. In fact, he didn't act any differently than usual. Still, it wouldn't be the first time that someone overlooked Maggie for Angel.

"What do you care? It isn't like you have feelings for Joshua. He's your boss. Mr. Whitfield's son. Sure, he's handsome, but he doesn't even read the books in the bookstore." She bit her lip after talking aloud to herself.

On the corner of Maple and Hershey Drive was a small sushi restaurant. Maggie went inside, found herself a quiet table in the corner, and took a seat. Next to her sat a bubbling fish tank with a dozen goldfish swimming around in it. She wondered if it bothered them to see the customers eating their aquatic brothers on rice with wasabi. She ordered herself a seaweed salad and the afternoon special that was a plate of delicious colorful samples of sushi.

As she looked out the window and slowly chewed her food, she pulled the receipt to Hawes Pawn Shop out of her pocket along with the bits of jewelry. The receipt was crinkled but had the date before Echo's body was found listed at the top. Maggie wondered if he was the one who stopped in. She'd find out soon enough.

Once her belly was full, Maggie didn't think she could make it to the pawn shop. Instead, she went home and waited for Angel. Once again, the endeavor was fruitless, since her sister had already left a note.

"Meeting with a friend. Won't be back until late. Please don't wait up," it said, signed with a heart and her name.

"I'm not a friend, I guess. Being a big sister is exhausting," Maggie said.

Chapter 13

Around noon the next day, the streets started lining with people. It was the Friday before the big fireworks display and dance that wrapped up the Fair Haven Centennial. This would be a grand parade with lots of foot traffic and excitement. Maggie felt terribly anxious. Maybe it was because large crowds made her feel awkward. Or maybe it was because she'd decided to go to Hawes Pawn Shop after work, and that had her stomach in nervous knots.

"We're just going to close up for about an hour," Joshua had said. "Then we'll open back up as the parade starts and—I hope—get a whole lot of visitors."

"Yeah," Maggie replied without looking at Joshua.

"Are you all right, Mags?"

"Yes. I'm fine," she replied as she pushed up her glasses and squinted. Of course, she wasn't. She wanted to ask him if he'd been palling around with Angel without even thinking to mention it. She felt a strong urge to ask him if he was interested in her. But when he tilted his head to the right and gave her a skeptical look from squinted eyes, she blushed.

"Yeah. If you say so. We'll talk later. It's been busy around here and out there." He jerked his thumb toward the bookstore door. "You and I have barely had any time to talk."

"Business has been good. Better than good. Your dad would be really proud, even if you did contaminate his shelves with *New York Times* best-sellers," Maggie added with a face like that of someone who'd just sucked a raw lemon.

"You're never going to forgive me for that, are you?" Joshua chuckled. His blond hair flopped over his forehead, and Maggie thought it was getting a little long along his ears.

"You need a haircut," she said and instantly wished she'd kept her mouth shut. Her cheeks burned, and she knew they were bright red.

"You think so? I was thinking I should grow it out a little, like that guy on the cover of all those romance novels," he said, pretending to flex his muscles. The burst of laughter that shot out of Maggie's mouth echoed through the bookstore and the café.

"Oh my gosh! What is so funny?" Babs asked as she came into the bookstore from the café side. She was holding a cup of coffee in her hands, looking like she just stepped out of a '50s drag-racing movie with her blond hair curled around her face and a bright turquoise scarf around her neck.

Maggie repeated what Joshua had said, making Babs laugh even harder as Joshua stood there, his hands on his hips and his eyes wide with shock.

"What's so funny?" he asked.

"You as a romance cover model," Babs blurted out in between giggles.

"What? You don't think I've got the stuff?" Joshua shook his hair and flipped it back dramatically. "I beg to differ."

"You would." Babs continued laughing as she went back into the café. Maggie smiled wide. She couldn't help herself, and when her eyes locked with Joshua's, she didn't shy away and look at the floor or tug at her sleeve. She tittered.

"That's better. I know you dole out your smiles like a miser parting with gold. But believe me, people want to see it. It looks nice," Joshua said before giving her a wink before walking to the back room of the bookstore.

She glowed for a couple seconds, but as usual, her self-doubt began to seep in. He was just being nice. He probably felt sorry for her. There was no harm in throwing a compliment to the homely girl at the dance. After a deep breath and a couple minutes looking outside at the faces who were admiring her display window, Maggie decided it was time to go pay Roger Hawes a visit.

"Babs, I'm going out to grab a bite before things go nuts around here," Maggie said and leaned into the café.

"Good idea, honey. See you in a little bit." Babs waved as she busied herself with cleaning the counter and coffee maker.

Maggie was sure the members of her sister's cult had stolen these items. Plus, if they were brought in by Echo, then maybe Maggie could figure out if Angel was with him before he got killed or after. If it was before, Angel would be in the clear. If it was after, well, it might be a little more difficult. But Maggie was sure her sister didn't kill anyone. At least not in cold blood. Self-defense maybe. Maybe.

Because of the overwhelming number of visitors and all the streets blocked off for the evening parade, Maggie found herself parking across the street from Patrick Cusic's garage. As she got out of her car and started to walk the block and a half to Hawes Pawn Shop, she could hear the man's voice bellowing inside.

"That is not what I told you to do! Here! Pick this up and do it again!" he shouted like a drill sergeant.

Maggie frowned and wondered what made him so angry all the time, although she refrained from thinking anything terribly bad about him. He did fix her car for her when it had been vandalized. Plus, the big palooka didn't even charge her. But that didn't change that the giant was as big and intimidating as a great white shark at lunchtime cruising a swimmer clinging to a Styrofoam noodle near the breakers.

She could see Patrick's shadow underneath a raised car fussing with something as a scrawny kid dashed back and forth, getting strange tools and gadgets for the colossal man to use. It was like he cast half the garage in darkness when he shifted his weight from one side to the other.

Maggie put her head down and quickened her pace past the garage. She didn't think Patrick would say anything to her. She wasn't interested in talking to him. But still, just his gigantic presence was enough to make her nervous. Just as she was out of view of the open mouth of the mechanic's shop, she heard something fall to the floor with a clang. A string of obscenities followed.

Hawes Pawn Shop was a long building that reminded Maggie of a sheet cake. Rectangular. Flat. Nothing special. Several windows stretched along the front of the building that was almost a block long. It had a flat roof. Iron gates covered each windowpane, making the building look like a small prison. The words Hawes Pawn Shop were painted on a faded billboard propped on top of the building facing traffic.

After a couple of deep breaths, Maggie walked up to the door and gave it a yank. It didn't open. People were inside. The neon sign that read Open was on and glowing. Maggie pressed her face against the glass cupping her hands around her eyes. Roger Hawes stared back at her like she was picking her nose as she gaped at his customers. The sound of a click and a buzzer were heard as the proprietor pressed a button behind the counter to unlock the door. Maggie gave it another good yank and stepped inside. A security guard sat on a stool to her left, and she smiled crookedly at him.

"This is an unexpected surprise," Roger Hawes said. "What are you doing here?"

"I came to talk to you about some business," Maggie replied as she fished through her pockets and found the crumpled receipt as well as the jewelry she'd swiped from Neal and Mike's hotel room.

The Hawes Pawn Shop was bright white on the inside. Several video cameras that recorded every bit of movement inside the place were mounted in the corners. In a U shape was a continuous counter that held so many gold and silver sparkly things Maggie was reminded of the vast hoard of treasure around the dragon in *The Hobbit*. And the harsh face of the owner certainly reminded Maggie of the dragon itself. She'd never been in Roger's shop. For some reason, she expected it to look more like a dusty, dirty, dryer version of Patrick Cusic's garage. Instead, it was clean with a light cologne in the air.

"Oh, yeah?"

"Yeah. Were these items stolen?" Maggie

blurted the words out then puffed her cheeks and wrinkled her nose before handing over the receipt.

Roger chuckled nervously as he looked at the two customers who had been turning over some jewelry themselves. Before he could reply, they grabbed their stuff, stuffed it into their pockets, and hurried out the door.

"What are you trying to do? Scare away my business?" Roger balked.

"What are you talking about?" Maggie asked.

"Look, Pollyanna, half the stuff that comes through the door has fallen off the back of a truck. I can't look into every item. I trust that my customers are telling me the truth when they bring something in to sell and sign the waiver that says it hasn't been stolen," Roger said, his voice sing-songy like he was speaking to a child. "People come to me because they need money. I'm doing a public service. I'm much more generous and nonjudgmental than the bank."

Maggie opened her mouth to speak, but Roger did have a point. Still, she couldn't be distracted from what she was there to discover.

"This receipt. Do you remember the guy who brought it in?" Maggie asked.

"No," Roger replied without even looking at it.

"Mr. Hawes, this is dated just one day before my sister's…husband…was found dead." Saying that word was like biting into ice cream and feeling it freeze her teeth.

"So," Roger replied, although Maggie could tell that it suddenly took on a little more weight than it had before.

"So if you saw the man who was killed at a certain time, it might help the police figure out who killed him. Don't you want to do *that* kind of public service by helping your local law enforcement?" Maggie asked.

"I mind my own business. In this business, that's the *only* business," Roger replied and pushed the receipt away from him.

"But an innocent person could be in trouble. Don't you want to help?"

"Who?" Roger folded his big, meaty arms across his chest and tilted his head to the right. He always looked like he needed a shave, and his salt-and-pepper hair looked a little greasy as it flipped in curls over his ears and stuck to his forehead.

After a deep sigh and a roll of her eyes, Maggie managed to answer. "My sister."

The deviant look that came over Roger's face made Maggie want to slap him like ladies did in the old days when a fellow did or said something inappropriate. But she'd have to stand on her tiptoes, reach over the counter, and hope he didn't shuck to the right or she'd lose her balance and tip over the counter.

"You've got a sister? Old or younger?" he asked.

"What does it matter? Look, I need you to tell me who you made this receipt out to." She pushed the receipt back toward Roger. He picked it up, a greasy smile still on his face before his eyes fell to the paper and read the description.

"A young woman and a young man brought in this inventory," he replied.

"What did she look like?" Maggie held her breath, hoping Roger would say a redhead with crossed eyes and a peg leg. But he described Angel right down to her silver charm.

"And what did the guy look like?" Maggie asked. She hadn't thought of this scenario, that her sister might have been in on the theft of people's things. It had to be against her will. She already admitted to Maggie that theft was one of the reasons she left the cult. They wanted her to steal. She just couldn't do it. Maggie believed her.

"Well, the man had long brown hair. His eyes

were a funny sort of green. Of course, that might have been since his eyes were so red," Roger said.

"What do you mean his eyes were so red?" Maggie asked.

"It looked like he had been crying or… more likely… was a little strung out. My guess was that they needed money for drugs."

"And you gave it to them?" Maggie stared, her mouth hanging open and her eyes wide.

"Like I said, I don't ask questions. I conduct business. That's all. That's why people trust me, right, Morice?" Roger yelled to the security guard who was still perched on the stool by the front door. He had sleepy eyes, but Maggie was confident nothing escaped them.

"That's right," Morice concurred.

"Did the girl… did she look like she was crying or on drugs?" Maggie asked.

Roger rolled his tongue around his mouth and watched Maggie closely before he answered. "No. No, she looked like she was completely levelheaded. She gave me the jewelry, and I gave her the money. As far as I know, when she stuffed it into those tight shorts, that was where it stayed." Maggie squinted at Roger and grimaced. "But she did have a bruise on her shoulder that was really big," Roger continued. "Or maybe it was a tattoo. You know how people like that want to look different. They crave attention."

Maggie pushed her glasses up on her nose. "Where is the jewelry they brought in?"

Roger walked behind the counter to the opposite end illuminated by a lot of natural light coming in from the windows. He tapped the glass and looked down. Maggie hurried over, and as soon as she saw the ring, a flash from her past sent a shiver up her spine. Why she didn't think of it when she first saw the simple description of an amethyst ring she didn't know. Perhaps she'd really forgotten about it. Maybe she just didn't want to remember it. But there it was, sparkling, clean and simple. The ring their father had given Angel when she turned sixteen. Maggie wasn't envious. On the contrary, she had one just like it with a ruby in it that she'd received for her sixteenth birthday. The ring was tucked in the corner of her jewelry box not far from the silver charm necklace. Again, it just wasn't her style. But the thought was still there. Since Angel was much closer to their father than Maggie ever was, the thought that she was pawning this ring broke her heart. She didn't care to see the other items on the list. They weren't stolen. Maggie could feel it. Perhaps they were something Angel had gotten for herself over the years. Maybe a gift from some lovestruck Romeo. Whatever they were, Maggie was sure Angel had come by them honestly.

"You interested in buying?" Roger asked.

Maggie looked at him with more disdain than he had when she entered the building. "You know I only work at the bookstore, Mr. Hawes. I couldn't possibly afford your prices."

"I'll give you a discount." He was trying to entice her but came across as desperate and a little creepy, like he was hoping his generosity might earn him a seat at the cool kids' table. When he looked Maggie up and down, she changed the subject quickly.

"Did they say anything?"

"Who?"

"My sister and the man she was with?" Maggie shook her head and looked like she'd smelled a skunk.

"They didn't say too much. But one guy came in just as soon as they left up. He was a real piece of work. Grayish hair. Beady eyes. His name was Grimes or Greasy or…"

"Grisham?"

"That's it. He wasn't from around here, but

we've been getting in all kinds in because of all the festivities. Good for business, but sometimes an unsavory element finds its way in. I didn't like that guy Grisham at all," Mr. Hawes said as he tugged at his collar as if it was becoming too snug around his thick neck. "You know him?"

"Only briefly. Did he bring you some jewelry too?" Maggie asked.

"No. He wasn't in the market to sell or buy. Instead, he was asking a lot of personal questions like how long I'd owned the place and how business was. He asked what kind of revenue you could expect to make running an establishment like mine. I don't like people who come in here asking a lot of questions. Isn't that right, Morice?" Roger gazed down at Maggie without looking at his security guard, who said yes immediately.

"I know lots of people who come in asking questions about how business is going and how long an establishment has been around. Not everyone is looking to pull the rug out from under you," Maggie said. Roger Hawes had done this exact thing several times a year to Mr. Whitfield when he was alive. Roger wanted to get his hands on the bookstore to expand his own enterprise. Thank goodness it didn't happen.

"Don't kid yourself, missy. I can smell a con artist a mile away. This guy Grisham was on a fishing exposition. I'm not sure what for, but he was casting a long line," Roger nodded.

"Did you tell him the other two had been in the store?" Maggie asked.

"Well, he did ask about some people who fit their description. I might have said something," Roger said as he scratched his chin.

"What? You just said the guy was fishing, and you didn't like people who fished and here you are helping him out," Maggie blustered.

"I thought maybe he was a concerned parent or relative or something. He said that he was looking for these people that fit your sister and her husband's description. They were members of his family," Roger said, rubbing the back of his neck.

"So much for smelling a con artist," Maggie snapped.

"Look, there was something odd about the guy. I didn't like how he looked. I just told the truth to get him out of my store," Roger stepped up closer to the counter to speak. "To be honest, he gave me the willies."

"Isn't that what you have Morice for?" Maggie jerked her thumb over her shoulder at the guard, who sat up at attention. Roger waved him down like he was chasing a lazy fly away. He leaned on the counter to get closer to Maggie. "He's more for show than anything else."

Maggie pinched her lips together before speaking. "That is the stupidest thing I've ever heard." With that, she grabbed the receipt and headed out of the pawn shop without even the slightest nod to poor Morice.

Chapter 14

It didn't feel like Maggie had been in the pawn shop for very long, but more people had crowded the streets, making her journey back to the bookstore slower than the one from it. The sounds of people happily chatting, bits of conversations, and bursts of laughter made her feel like the only one with a problem.

She felt she was going in circles. Nothing indicated that Angel had done anything wrong, but still, Echo was dead, and whether she was his *wife* legitimately or not, she'd be the prime suspect. The sound of fire engines and police sirens could be heard several blocks away as the parade was about to get underway.

Maggie continued to walk and tried to enjoy the excitement. But the smiles on everyone's faces and the cheery atmosphere made her feel anxious. She caught a glimpse of a squirrel dashing up one side of a tree with another in hot pursuit then they both circled down, around, and finally back up the tree out of sight. That was exactly how Maggie felt. She was running after Angel, who was all over the place, but neither of them knew where they were going.

Music was being piped through the speakers that lined the main downtown streets, a treat usually reserved for Christmastime when the snow was falling, and locals would donate ice sculptures of angels and reindeer to adorn the corners. Today, Maggie could hear the proud sounds of an orchestra playing *The Battle Hymn of the Republic* floating underneath the bustle on the street. A popcorn vendor on the street made almost the entire block smell of the warm, buttery snack.

An ice cream truck was also parked off the main drag, surrounded by kids with their parents eagerly hopping up and down as they pointed at the sign, identifying what cold dessert would be best on this warm evening. Maggie smiled but still wrinkled her face. This proved it. She was the only person in all of Fair Haven with a problem. Before she could even laugh at herself or find something to give her hope, she saw a sight across the street that made her gut seize up into a knot. Gary was talking with Angel, and neither of them was smiling. He had his notebook out, and it was obvious from Angel's body language that she was not happy. Her hands were waving around like she was trying to give directions.

Maggie went to cross the street, but the wooden horses were in the way. To keep the celebrations safely out of the line of the slow-moving traffic, which included the mayor's convertible and some of the farmer's giant green John Deere tractors that moved at a heart-racing three miles an hour, police and volunteers were positioned every couple of yards to keep the masses back. Maggie didn't care. She went to skirt around one of the wooden barriers but was caught quickly.

"Miss! Miss! You can't cross here! You have to go to the corner!" ordered a man who wore blue jeans and a blue shirt with the word Volunteer in yellow letters on the back. Maggie looked at him with a wrinkled nose and pushed up her glasses. "You can't cross here!"

"I heard you the first time," she muttered as she felt

the eyes of the people around her giving her a judgmental stare. Just as she was about to walk down the block and out of her way, she saw the volunteer turn his back and begin a conversation with another person. Within seconds they were walking away, their backs to Maggie. She quickly ducked under the wooden horse.

"Daddy, that lady is going around the fence," she heard some little kid say.

"She's going to get in trouble," another chimed in.

Without looking back Maggie hurried across the street to where Angel was standing with Gary. Angel's face looked strained and tired.

"Funny seeing you guys here. It's like finding a needle in a haystack," Maggie said and looked across the street to see the volunteer glaring at her with his arms folded. She quickly looked at Angel. "What's up?"

"Maggie, would you talk to your sister and tell her I have a job to do? I'm not accusing her of anything," Gary said, his eyes hard and determined as he watched Angel's reaction.

"It sure seems like you are," Angel said as she folded her arms over her chest. Maggie thought her baby sister looked especially cute in her shorts and a plain pink T-shirt until she realized the T-shirt was hers.

"Where did you get that shirt?" Maggie asked.

"Out of your dresser," Angel replied. "I didn't think you'd mind."

"Well, I don't mind, but it would have been nice if you had asked first." Maggie touched the hem of the short sleeve.

"You weren't wearing it. In fact, it still had a price tag on it," Angel snapped.

"That doesn't make it yours," Maggie volleyed back.

"Maggie, can you please help me out?" Gary interrupted.

"Oh, yeah. Whatever Gary is doing, you can trust him. He's a good guy," Maggie said before squinting her eyes and tugging at the hem of her own blouse. She and Angel were almost the same size. But where Angel liked things to be slightly tighter and shorter, Maggie preferred a more modest style.

"I feel like I need a lawyer before I talk to this guy," Angel replied.

"No. Why would you say that? Why would she say something like that, Gary?" Maggie looked at the man who had been her friend since high school and who had gone out of his way to make her feel comfortable, as if he was the only one who understood she might have been uncomfortable.

"Maggie, I am investigating a possible murder case," Gary said, his eyebrows pinched together as he shrugged. "You know I can't exclude anyone. I've got people who say they saw Angel with the deceased before he… became deceased." Judging by the way he shifted from one leg to the other, Maggie knew he didn't like what he was doing. Still, she knew it was his job, but it still bothered her he was treating her sister as a common suspect. Maybe handling her with kid gloves might be more appropriate.

"I know how things go in these small towns. Any outsiders are instantly targeted and blamed for everything that goes wrong. It's no different from witch trials. Your crops aren't growing, so blame it on the new woman who came to town. Don't think it might be because you don't know how to farm," Angel hissed.

"Come on, Angel. No one thinks, that do they, Gary?" Maggie looked at Officer Brookes, whose expression reminded her of the stone *Thinker* that had a perplexed expression on its mug for all eternity.

"See?" Angel replied.

"Gary, you can't possibly think that Angel had anything to do with Echo's death. She was his wife, for heaven's sake," Maggie blurted out to help—but the looks of astonishment on both Gary and Angel's faces made her realize she had really stepped in it.

"Is this true?" Gary asked.

"We were only married in the community. It wasn't official. There was no justice of the peace or a priest or anything. Grisham did it. I don't think it counted," Angel stammered. "Don't look at me like that, Mags."

"It's true, then." Maggie couldn't hide her disappointment. Not to mention that this was one more nail in her sister's coffin. The spouse was always the prime suspect. "Why didn't you tell me sooner?"

"Look at how you are reacting now. Do you think it would have been better if I told you later?" Angel replied.

"Probably not." Maggie pinched her lips together and looked at Gary. "Like she said, it was done by their cult leader. It isn't a binding contract." Maggie had expected to see Gary nod. But he didn't. Instead, his eyes narrowed as he looked at Angel and began to scribble more notes in his notepad.

"Angel, how long had you and Echo been married?" Gary inquired.

"Wait a minute. You can't possibly think that makes her more of a suspect. I mean, that whole group of weirdos… any one of them could have done away with Echo. He could have been needling someone for weeks. Have you questioned all of them like you are my sister?" Maggie unconsciously stepped between Gary and Angel.

"I've questioned a few of them, yes," Gary replied. "Maggie. You aren't helping."

Those words made Maggie feel personally insulted. He wasn't just a cop doing his job. He was Gary. They were friends. She thought he was handsome and kind and sweet, even if she'd never told him such. But here he was, putting his job before their friendship. That wasn't what real men did. Real men defended you come hell or high water.

Come on, Mags. You know he's got a job to do. He can't worry about feelings or histories. He's got to get to the bottom of this case. Maggie's thoughts were harsh. Who did she pledge her allegiance to? The guy who came to her rescue more than once or her sister, who shared some of the same blood but was already up to stealing her T-shirts without permission?

"Is my sister under arrest?" Maggie asked.

"No. Not at this time," Gary said as if the next time she might be. Maybe it was how the light fell on his face or because he'd probably been working hard since the sun came up, but Maggie saw a very different look on his face than she'd ever seen before. Gary looked angry.

"You can't tell what happened at this early stage," Maggie said. "What does the autopsy say? Maybe there was something else. Maybe…"

"The body was sent to Odell. Our medical examiner is out for two weeks on a fishing trip. They haven't finished yet, but it's pretty clear that…"

Maggie reached down without looking and took her sister's hand. "Then I think she's done talking to you for tonight, Gary," Maggie replied and pulled Angel along behind her like they used to do when they were so much younger.

As they walked, Angel didn't let go. Maggie couldn't help feeling nostalgic. She'd spent some times playing dolls with and reading books to Angel. Angel seemed so much more manageable back in those days. Or was it that Maggie was more flexible back then?

"What did he ask you?" Maggie asked as they stopped in the park under a huge oak tree. The people strolled past them without paying any attention to the looks of worry on Maggie's face and her sister's eye-rolling.

"Just a lot of nonsense. Nothing important," Angel replied.

"Nothing important? Angel, please. You are a suspect in a murder. This isn't just leaving the Great Society of Atonement cult. This is serious." Maggie squeezed her sister's hand tightly.

"You think I did it. You think I killed him," Angel said.

"Did you? Because the way you are acting tells me you are hiding something. Did the people in the GSA put you up to it? Grisham? Did he convince you that this had to be done?" Maggie saw Angel's body shake at the mention of Grisham's name.

"You read too many books. That's always been your problem. I'm not some character in a book, Mags. No hero is going to swoop in and save the day. The bad guy isn't going to get his comeuppance. I'm a real person with feelings who makes mistakes, and you never were able to understand that." The tip of Angel's nose became red as tears filled her eyes.

"And you haven't read enough to know that you are a poster child for someone who has been through trauma. You said Echo wasn't nice to you. If you took matters into your own hands… Angel, no one would blame you for that. No one. But you've got to be honest with me. I'm your sister. I can help."

Angel sniffled and wiped her nose on the back of her hand. "Half sister. I'll be leaving tomorrow morning."

Those words broke Maggie's heart. How many times had she referred to Angel that way? What had she been thinking? Was she so envious of Angel that she took those little shots at her? Her mouth went dry. She couldn't find any words to soothe her sister. It wasn't just one comment that made her mad. It was a lifetime of snarky remarks and condescending comments.

"You can't leave. You'll be on the lam. They'll think you are guilty for sure if you leave now. Angel, trust me. Stay a little while longer. No matter what happens, I'll help you. Even if that means helping you sneak away," Maggie said and meant it. But her offer to help Angel avoid being taken into custody didn't seem to help soothe her sister's heart.

Angel looked off into the distance as if something at the end of the park had caught her attention, and she squinted to see it more clearly. When she did that, Maggie saw herself in her sister's face. They were so much more than half sisters. Why did it take so long for Maggie to see that?

"Fine. I'll be home late," Angel said just above a whisper and quickly walked away.

Maggie didn't chase after her. It was no use. They both needed a little space. Maggie looked at the crowd that lined the street as a massive red fire truck slowly rolled past. Men in their blue uniforms with red suspenders tossed candy to the kids. In between were pickup trucks and pulling floats for the hardware store and one of the insurance companies that was in town. The sound of a live band playing "*Stars and Stripes Forever*" could be heard a way off and slowly approaching.

Everyone seemed to be having a good time. But like usual, Maggie felt annoyed and isolated. Why couldn't she just go up to the street and enjoy the parade like everyone else? Her sister didn't kill anyone. That notion was so ludicrous it was almost laughable. Why was she so worried? Did she know something about her sister that would make murder even a possibility?

"Of course not," she muttered. "She's just flaky. That's all. There is no law against being flaky." Maggie squinted as she walked back to the book-store. As she continued to mumble to herself, shake her head, and occasionally wave her arms, she repeated her mantra. *There is no law against being flaky.*

Chapter 15

The following day, the streets of Fair Haven were even more crowded as more and more visitors came to enjoy the celebration of the town's establishment. Maggie had to park six blocks away and had worn a festive red skirt with a white blouse to get into the spirit of things. But it was nearly impossible. Angel didn't come home.

Maggie lay in bed most of the night listening for any noise that would indicate the girl was sneaking in. But everything remained quiet. Painfully quiet. She got up a few times and peeked out the window into Mrs. Peacock's backyard. The soft glow of her decorative lights made the landscape look like something out of an old sci-fi film.

Perhaps a UFO had landed, or maybe little green men were altering the terrain with mellow laser lights. Nothing stirred. She picked up her phone more than once to make sure there was a dial tone, and the lines hadn't gone out for some reason. Maybe the little green men cut all lines of communication before they invade.

"Have you never heard of a phone, Angel?" Maggie snapped into the darkness. She sat in her parlor, just waiting to see her sister's familiar shadow walk past to the front door. But there was nothing. The worst part was that Maggie didn't know whether she should be angry or scared. She tried to make a deal with the Almighty that if her sister came home in the next five minutes, she wouldn't yell at her. She wouldn't even confront her. She'd calmly ask where she was and why she didn't call. But five minutes came and went. Then another five and another. Finally, Maggie's tired shoulders and back told her to go lie down.

When she woke up, she hurried to peek at the couch where Angel had been sleeping, but it was completely undisturbed. The idea of calling Gary had crossed her mind. However, if Angel had decided to skip town, the least Maggie could do was give her enough of a head start that she might be able to get away. Clear her head before she made any drastic decisions.

As the morning crept along and Maggie got ready, she worried more and more. The problem was that this was not unusual behavior for her sister. Angel had a way of just doing things her own way. Could she have just spent the night at some man's house or maybe even on a park bench? Sure. But she could also be dead in a ditch somewhere. This whole scenario was an example of an epic move of selfishness.

Maggie left a note on her door. "CALL ME AT THE BOOKSTORE THE SECOND YOU GET THIS," it read. That the message was written in all caps should have been enough of an indication that Maggie was upset and Angel had some apologizing to do. That was all Maggie could think of on her way to work. Did she want to just accept Angel's apology and move on like it didn't happen, like she wasn't awake all night and now exhausted in the morning after worrying? Or did she want to give Angel the silent treatment in an attempt to teach her a lesson that you couldn't behave like a teenager and expect to be treated like an adult?

What if she didn't show up at the store? What if, like Echo, she'd gone missing and would be the next person found at the bottom of the Hickory Creek Bridge? Maggie tried to push those thoughts out of her head. Her sister had to be all right. She'd never forgive herself if anything had happened to her baby sister. Just as she approached the bookstore, she felt a sting of tears in her eyes.

"Where could she be?" She blinked her eyes rapidly while she fumbled for her keys to open the store.

As she struggled with the keys to the front door of the shop, the familiar words of The Bookish Café looking back at her, she was able to see inside. What was there made her heart catch in her throat. It was Angel. She wore an oversized T-shirt. Her legs and feet were bare. And she was standing toe to toe with Joshua. He was looking down at her and smiling as she looked up at him adoringly.

Maggie felt a lump form in her throat. It was too late to stop herself. She shoved the key in the lock and jimmied the mechanism to alert the pair that she was there and also to release some of the anger, disappointment, shock, and jealousy that had swooped down on her from out of nowhere.

When she finally got the door open, Joshua and Angel turned and looked at her. Angel's face turned bright red before she went up the stairs to the apartment that Joshua had been living in since his father's death.

"Good morning," Joshua said as he thrust his hands into his front denim pockets and pulled his shoulders up around his ears. "You're here early."

"I guess I am," she said and hurried around the counter. Maggie was shredded on the inside. But instead of demanding to know why her sister was there and wearing nothing but a baggy T-shirt Maggie assumed was Joshua's, she bit her tongue, literally, tossed around her purse and a few books and the bank bag, and pounded the keys on the register just to avoid looking at him.

"Look, Maggie, I think you need to know…"

"I don't need to know anything. I've got to get to the bank," she replied. With the pouch in her hand, she began to stuff the previous days' sales inside along with the receipts.

"Wait. I've got something I want to share with you and… I think you are going to be very happy," Joshua replied and looked over his shoulder in the direction Angel had been.

"Is my sister moving in with you?" Maggie asked.

"Is your sister… what?"

"Come on, Joshua. Do you think I didn't see her

just now? Are you out of your mind? She was wearing your shirt." Maggie bit down harder on her tongue to stop the emotions from surfacing in her eyes.

"Yes… uhm… she was but…"

"This is too much. She's a suspect in a murder, and still everyone can overlook it like she did nothing more than get a speeding ticket. I've got to get to the bank. Am I still employed here at the bookstore?" Maggie asked and squinted at Joshua before pouting.

"Maggie, of course you are. Why, this wouldn't be the Bookish Café without you." He took a step forward just as Maggie stepped aside, clutched the bank pouch to her chest, and headed toward the door.

"Fine. I'll be back after I drop this at the bank."

"Maggie, you aren't making sense," Joshua said. "I said I needed to talk to you."

"And I said I have to get to the bank. It can wait," she snapped.

"Now hold on. I know we kind of blur the lines a bit on authority in this place. I kind of like that there are no hard and fast rules. But I am the boss. This is my bookstore and…"

"Right. And if I don't get the money from last

night into the account, it will screw up the payday and bill-paying schedule. And don't forget that you owe that guy who wore too much cologne for the new fixtures in the bathroom." Maggie prattled away about half a dozen other obligations to Joshua, real and imagined, before exiting the store and leaving him stupefied and annoyed. She reached the bank without seeing any of the scenery or hearing any people. The image of her sister in Joshua's clothes and so blatantly staying at his apartment over the store, the apartment where her beloved boss, Mr. Alexander Whitfield, had lived a simple life of sipping tea and reading his books, complete with his old-fashioned fireplace and comfy armchair. Maggie wondered if her sister had been playing her for a fool like she had with Echo. Had she and Joshua been laughing at her behind her back, too?

You are jumping to conclusions. You don't know anything, her conscience said, trying to pull her head out of the clouds. It was no use. Maggie was angry and disappointed and *envious*. That was the worst part. She envied her baby sister.

"This is ridiculous. I should be past all of this. We are two completely different people. Not one better than the other. Except that everyone always seems to think she is wonderful. They let her get away with everything. And she's prettier and smaller and says what she thinks and leads with her heart and never seems to get hurt except..." Maggie's last mumble hung in her throat like a fish caught on a hook. She looked up to see Wilma DeForest, the only teller at the bank she could tolerate, staring right at her. The bank employees knew more about what was going on around town than Sheriff Smith or the rest of Fair Haven's law enforcement. In lowered voices and with cupped hands, they'd swap information like recipes. If anyone wanted to know what was going on with who in town, all they had to do was come and make a deposit.

"You okay, Maggie?" At the mention of her name, all the other tellers who weren't assisting customers peeked in their direction. It was all because of Joshua Whitfield. He was the hottest commodity in Fair Haven, and Maggie worked with him. In seconds, Joyce appeared like magic out of nowhere.

"Yes." Maggie stomped up to the window and pushed her glasses up her nose. "Last night's receipts. Can you give me a stack of deposit slips too?"

"Of course. So, how are things at the book-store?" Wilma asked innocently.

"Fine," Maggie replied.

"Maggie, are you going to the fireworks display tomorrow?" Joyce asked, wondering only because she thought if Maggie was there Joshua might be there.

"No," Maggie replied and shook her head, pouting.

"You're not? The whole town is going to be there," Wilma replied. "It will be fun."

"No. Can I get those deposit slips?" She tried to hurry Wilma along, but like a good small-town resident, Wilma couldn't just let a familiar face go without a little gossip.

"I heard about the trouble with that group of people who came to town. The one young man who turned up dead, I heard he was a friend of yours," Wilma said, her voice only slightly lowered.

"No," Maggie said, her eyes barely reaching Wilma's collar.

"You didn't know him?"

"My sister knew him. I only met him once or twice," Maggie replied.

"Did the police talk to your sister about him? That group has been wandering through town passing out pamphlets and wishing everyone love and happiness. I thought those kinds of groups went out with bell bottoms. I was suspicious of them in those days, and I still am," Wilma said with a huff.

"But the members in those days weren't as good-looking as this bunch," one of the other tellers chirped, making everyone titter but Maggie.

"So, you aren't going to the fireworks?" Joyce asked. "Is…"

"Is Joshua going? I don't know," Maggie replied and forced a quick smile that was more a crooked grimace than anything else.

Joyce narrowed her eyes and continued to stare at Maggie as if she was hiding something. Finally, Wilma returned Maggie's money pouch and was grabbing a stack of deposit slips when she spoke.

"I do hope your sister chooses better friends in the future. Seems a lot of stuff shows up missing when they are around," Wilma replied.

"What do you mean by that?" Maggie asked as she slowly took the deposit forms and stared at Wilma.

Wilma looked over her shoulder before slightly leaning forward and folding her arms on the counter in front of her. "I have a friend who works at the Copper Tower Hotel."

Maggie swallowed hard and stared at Wilma.

"She said those people are getting free rooms because they took the manager into their confidence and whispered a couple words of hocus pocus on the guy, and he's comped their entire stay," Wilma said, clearing her throat.

"Really? I heard they threatened him," Maggie replied.

"Oh, no. They are all about peace and stuff. But it seems that there are a quite a few people on staff who feel the whole group has sticky fingers. They come in with no luggage to speak of, no reservation, no nothing, and over the course of a couple days have gotten new clothes, fancy shoes, and even some jewelry. Where are they getting the money?"

Maggie reached out to take the slips, but they were just beyond her grasp. She looked at Wilma and squinted.

"How am I supposed to know? I'm not in that cult," Maggie snapped.

"No. But if your sister is, maybe…" Wilma dropped her chin, looked up from beneath her thinning eyelashes, and blinked.

"Maybe what?" Maggie continued to squint.

The grin on Wilma's face quickly dropped. She realized she'd overstepped her bounds and quickly handed Maggie the deposit slips. Maggie snatched them from Wilma's hand and shoved them inside the cash bag.

"I'm sorry, Maggie." Wilma had realized she'd overstepped her bounds.

"My sister isn't in that cult anymore. She's trying to get away, and they followed her. It's sad, not something for you to poke fun at." Maggie scowled at Wilma and all the other women within earshot.

Joyce retreated into her office. As she nervously fussed with the zipper, Maggie pinched her lips together before turning and walking away.

Why did she even defend her sister? Angel had never done that for her.

Mags, what have you ever done that required her to come to your defense? So she didn't do it once. That hardly constitutes a pattern of behavior.

She twisted her mouth in annoyance at her own thoughts. This was just too much. It seemed like since Angel arrived, everyone was looking at the two of them all the time. Maggie looked down and watched the cracks in the sidewalk as she walked. She saw gum from a year ago, pink and flat. A couple of cigarette butts lay on the ground, and Maggie thought how much she hated cigarette smoke, but something about smelling it outside around a carnival or summer festivities like these was rather romantic. There was a small shard of glass and a green weed squeezing through a tiny slit. Before she realized it, she collided into a person coming from the other direction, nearly falling to the ground.

"Oww!" She put her hand to her head and looked at the human obstacle in her way. Normally she would have been happy to see this person but not today.

"Didn't you hear me calling your name as you got closer?" Gary asked.

Chapter 16

Maggie shook her head and put her hands on her hips. "So you took that to mean I wanted you to walk right into me."

"You were marching like you were going off to war. If I didn't get in the way, who knows what kind of damage you might have done to some innocent pedestrian?" Gary grinned.

"I don't know if there is a such a thing as an innocent pedestrian where you are concerned." Maggie struck first but didn't feel an ounce of regret.

"What is that supposed to mean?"

"You were grilling my sister yesterday as if she was the one who pushed Echo off that bridge. You know she couldn't have done it," Maggie said on tiptoe close to Gary's ear.

With the gossip mill working overtime at the bank, the last thing Maggie wanted to do was add to it. In her mind everyone knew who Angel was and, through association, knew who Maggie was. If she had to put money on it, she'd bet they all thought Angel had done it. Even Gary.

"I don't know that, Mags. But I'm doing everything I can to get her crossed off the list," Gary replied just as softly.

"And? What have you found out?" Maggie stared at him over the top of her glasses. She was instantly sorry she asked as he looked to the left and then down at his shoes before meeting her eyes.

"Has Angel ever had a history of drug use?"

"Why do people keep asking that?"

"Well, has she?"

"No. Of course not. She's flaky and free-spirited, but she's no junkie. Why are you even asking me that question?" Maggie asked.

Gary retrieved the pad of paper he always kept in his breast pocket and flipped over a couple of pages. When he stopped, he took a deep breath and began to read.

"The night before Echo Mann's body was

found, he and your sister were seen in Hopland's Drugstore. Later that night, someone broke into the place," Gary said.

"So? What does that have to do with Angel? How many other people were in the drugstore that night? Are you questioning them?" Maggie asked.

"The half prescription we found on Echo's person was for Halcion," Gary said. Maggie shrugged and shook her head, lifting her hands palms up at her sides before letting them fall back down. She was getting tired of listening.

"Halcion helps people with insomnia. It's also very addictive," Gary replied.

"So are you saying someone killed Echo because he was cranky?"

"No, Mags. I'm saying that was what was stolen from the drugstore along with a bottle of Chantix," Gary replied as if he expected Maggie to snap her fingers, roll her eyes, and shout "*That's it!*" She stared at him blankly.

"That sounds like a real stretch, Gary."

"Did your sister smoke?"

"I think she did when she was younger, but I'm pretty sure she quit. She doesn't smell like she smokes. Gary, this is all wonderful information that you are passing along, but it has nothing to do with my sister."

"Chantix is known to cause violent outbursts in the people who take it. Not just shouting or being snippy. Full-on blind rage. Blind rage, Maggie." Gary looked at her. "If your sister was taking this stuff, and she and Echo got into a fight while he was on medication to make him drowsy, and she was angry, she might not even remember doing anything to him."

Maggie felt like she'd been punched in the gut. "Is this true? I've heard of Chantix. I think I read a couple things about it from some of Mr. Whitfield's science magazines. Nothing ever said it made people violent."

"I'm not saying that the case is closed, Maggie. But I need you to help me. Angel won't talk to me. She won't answer any questions in anything other than vague, confrontational responses. She's hiding something," Gary said.

"My sister would never steal. Especially not drugs. You are looking in the wrong place. Why don't you go and ask the members of the cult that followed her to town how they are paying for their clothes and food and everything else?" Maggie replied, lifting her chin. "Love and peace? They were what Jim Jones promoted too."

"What do you know about them?" Gary asked. Maggie swallowed hard. She didn't want to say too much and get her sister in any more trouble. But at the same time, she'd heard them talking about Echo and his money and how they were stealing and pawning what they collected.

"I know they want my sister back with them. They don't think she killed Echo, or else why would they want her back in the fold? Right?" Maggie asked.

"Where is she now?"

Maggie swallowed hard as the image of her sister with Joshua resurfaced. For a few precious seconds, she'd forgotten about it. All this talk about drugs and robberies had given her a respite from the disappointment in her heart.

"She's at the bookstore. I think Joshua let her stay there last night," Maggie said.

When she looked at Gary, his expression didn't shift at all, which let her know he was as shocked as she was. Unlike the people he pulled aside for questioning, Maggie could read Gary's poker face.

"All right. I'm going to go and try to talk to her there. I want you to come with and…" Just then,

Gary's radio went off. Some kind of fight was going on outside a bar that had closed over five hours ago. Maggie recognized the name.

"What's that?" she asked.

"Your favorite tavern is having a little trouble getting people to leave after last call at three a.m. Apparently there's a fight in the parking lot with a couple of the patrons. Do you want to come? Maybe some of the folks at Little Al's will listen to you. I'm sure they haven't forgotten you."

Maggie pushed up her glasses and, for the first time in what felt like weeks, smiled. She had been at Little Al's place, a bar for seasoned drinkers. Something she was not. And word spread quickly that Maggie Bell had had a little too much to drink at that establishment, nearly needing to be carried out after fifteen minutes.

"I don't know why you are bringing that up. You weren't there." Maggie cleared her throat and pushed up her glasses.

"I've got to go," Gary replied with a wink. "I'm trying to help your sister. Can you talk to her for me?"

Maggie nodded. Gary left her standing alone on the sidewalk.

Maggie had to talk to Angel about everything,

and if it meant tying the girl to a chair and making her listen, she was going to do that. Angel was still her sister. She had to warn her that Gary wanted to question her about the drugs.

But like with every well-thought-out plan, a wrench was always lying around somewhere for someone to throw into the works. When Maggie finally got back to the bookstore, she stomped in like a tax collector out of a Dickens novel. Joshua stood still, like an angry hornet had just landed on his arm.

"Where is my sister?" Maggie tossed the bank bag on the counter.

"Maggie, I know what you are thinking, and you are totally wrong." Joshua put his hands up as though surrendering.

"I'm thinking I need to talk to my sister. She promised me she was going to stay until this whole thing was settled. Where is she?" Maggie folded her arms and pinched her lips together.

"Angel told me she was going to the park to enjoy the last day of the fair. The fireworks are tonight. Are you going?" Joshua asked, his eyebrows raised.

"Am I going to the fireworks? No. But Joyce at the bank is and wants to show you some of her own. So why don't you go with her?" Maggie had no idea where those words came from or how they travelled so quickly from her mind to her mouth. But they were out, and there was no getting them back. So, with a flourish, Maggie yanked the door open.

"Wait. Where are you going?" Joshua asked.

"I need to find my sister," she snapped. But before she walked out the door, she looked at Joshua. "She's in trouble, and I can help. Can I go look for her?"

There might have been an elephant in the room, but Joshua was still Maggie's boss, even if she had a crush on him and he had one on her sister. It wasn't a matter of Maggie needing the money and the job. It was a matter of respect.

"Of course, you can. But be careful, and if I don't hear back from you in an hour, I'm coming to get you. If I have to close the bookstore and lose all the sales, I will," Joshua said with a smirk.

Maggie mustered an embarrassed grin and felt her cheeks flush. Before he could see her blush, she looked down and walked out. It was barely ten o'clock, and Maggie felt like she was ready to call it a day.

"Now, where would she be?" Maggie stood at

the edge of the park. Already it was bustling with people, vendors were making a pretty penny from all the tourists and out-of-towners, and food was starting to sizzle on the outdoor grills from picnickers and restauranteurs. The faint sound of music came from deep inside the perimeter.

"Maybe she's by the band," Maggie muttered. It was as good a place to start as any. Maggie stepped into the grass and regretted it instantly. The dew was still on the ground and saturated her canvas Mary-Jane style shoes. She detested the feeling, a shiver of disgust running through her body. Now her feet would feel cold and clammy all day.

But it's for Angel, she told herself. The thought didn't comfort her. She took a deep breath and sought out the sidewalk that wove its way around the park. However, as she headed in that direction, a strange flash of movement caught in the reflection of her glasses. Someone was close behind her. Too close.

Pretending nothing was out of the ordinary, Maggie decided to check to ensure she wasn't just paranoid and that someone was following her trail. Without another thought to the wet grass, she darted to the right to look over a table of leather pocketbooks. Then, without warning, she went to the left to peek at some hand-painted postcards. Sure enough, there was someone shadowing her.

Instructions from her childhood popped into her head. "If you are away from home and someone is following you, find a police officer or a woman with children and tell them you are in trouble." Maggie didn't see either. Casually, she started to walk to the most crowded part of the park. She wasn't sure who was behind her, but whoever it was wanted either her or Angel. That narrowed it down to any one of the members of the Greater Society of Atonement.

Finally, after a couple of additional steps and a burst of courage, Maggie stopped and whirled around to catch Grisham, Neal, and Mike. Grisham was trying to turn his head and hide his face. Too late. He realized it was no use. He'd been spotted. He didn't run. He didn't scowl. Instead, he waved and gave an innocent shrug as if he had just been playing a game.

"Maggie!" he called out to her as if they were friends.

Like a deer in the headlights, she froze. Grisham approached her with the kindest smile on his face that she'd ever seen. It was like a mask. Had he not been the head of the Greater Society of Atonement, he would have more than likely been a politician. Obviously, he could talk out of both sides of his mouth, making promises he never intended to keep while offering solutions to problems he was going to make.

"Hi, Maggie," he said as if he'd been waiting to talk to her. "You look really nice today."

"What do you want?"

"Your sister is in trouble," Grisham said, standing dangerously close her. "I need to know where she is so I can help her."

"I'm her family. I'll take care of her," Maggie replied as she felt her cheeks get red with anxiety. She wrinkled her nose, pushed her glasses up, and then folded her arms across her chest. Grisham chuckled.

"You can't help her the way I can." Grisham smiled condescendingly, making Maggie itch like a creepy-crawly had scurried across her bare skin. "But maybe you can help me. I know you'd like to do that. Angel, she's been telling you things about us. They aren't true. We love her. We all do. Unconditionally. But we think she's done a bad thing."

"My sister didn't have anything to do with Echo's death," Maggie hissed.

"Are you sure? Have you asked her that? Did she give you an honest answer, or did she hesitate and look to the left for a second before answering you? Did you know she had a motive?" Grisham purred. "I know it. I know all about Angel. And I know that she was desperate and scared and afraid to come to me. I could have helped her before things got so out of hand."

"From what I could tell, you let things get out of hand. Angel came back to me the night Echo died with scratches on her. What did you know about that?" Maggie felt her blood start to boil as Grisham smirked and rolled his eyes like she was pointing out a silly detail that meant nothing.

"I know that Angel bought drugs for Echo," Grisham said. "He had trouble sleeping—and other things. He'd worn out his welcome with some of the local doctors who wouldn't prescribe to him anymore. Angel helped him."

"I don't believe you. Angel would never do that. If Echo was addicted to something, she would have tried to help. If I know my sister, and I think I do, she'd have come to you and asked for help." Then

Maggie saw the glint in Grisham's eye. She'd hit the nail on the head. "She did, didn't she. And you didn't help her. You didn't want Echo to get help because he wouldn't be as easy to control. He had something you wanted, didn't he?"

Grisham swallowed hard but kept that smirk frozen on his lips. It was not a pleasant look, and behind his blue eyes Maggie could see the heat of disapproval flickering there. She remembered the conversation between Neal and Mike about the money Echo came from. Suddenly, she realized why they wanted Angel. If Echo and she were married, and it was slightly legal, perhaps Angel stood to inherit some sum of cash. And they weren't going to let her go if there was a trust fund baby financing their group.

But they were getting a hotel stay for nothing. They were stealing left and right then pawning the stuff all over town. Or at least trying to. What did they need Echo's money for unless they were living beyond their means? It could have been as simple as that. But Maggie didn't care what their motivation was. Angel was not going back with them.

"Yes, Echo had something you wanted. And now it's Angel's. And you think you can convince

her that you have her best interests at heart?"
Maggie chuckled.

"Oh, like you do? She told me all about you,
Margaret. How you were awkward and buried your
head in a book every chance you got while she was
gaining attention and popularity. You never cared
about Angel. Perhaps it's you who wants something
from your sister," Grisham said. "You are so obviously in pain. I can help you. If you'll help me. It's
so simple to walk in the light, to feel the warmth of
people who don't just love you but accept you the
way you are. Isn't that what you always wanted,
Maggie? To be accepted the way you are and not
considered an embarrassment because of your
eclectic taste and style."

Unbeknownst to Grisham, Maggie had read
more than one book on mind manipulation and
hypnosis. Mr. Whitfield had collected an extensive
library of books on cults, their leaders, and the
methods they used to gain followers. Grisham was a
bargain-basement version of those cult leaders who
made history through their cruel governance. He
was no Jim Jones or Charles Manson or that weird
guy who had his followers convinced they were
going to be picked up by aliens once they all killed

themselves. In Maggie's opinion, Grisham was nothing more than a wannabe. No, he clearly had a different motivation, and it was plain, old-fashioned greed. But his focus had shifted to Angel, and Maggie was not going to let him get to her.

"Did my sister tell you how smart I am and that I can tell a fraud when I see one?" Maggie asked. Although she was proud of herself for standing up to Grisham, she suddenly thought this might not have been the correct time or place to do such a thing. Grisham's jaw clenched, and his smirk became more of a snarl. He snatched out his hand to grab her but wasn't quick enough.

Maggie shook her head and started to back up.

"No, wait." He put out his hands as if that was somehow a comforting gesture that would convince her he didn't intend to do her any harm. No, he had no intention of grabbing her, tossing her into the back of an unmarked van, tying her up, and slipping a pillowcase over her head so she'd have no idea where she was going before they started their brainwashing techniques. Those thoughts rained down on Maggie with lightning speed, and she turned and ran.

"Wait! I need to talk to you!" Grisham called

out, still waving and smiling as Mike and Neal split up, obviously to corral her like a wayward calf.

Maggie began to speed walk through the crowd. She hated how she had to get off the sidewalk and into the dewy grass in an attempt to give them all the slip. Her shoes were soaked, even though it was a deliciously warm day. The smell of hot food cooking on open grills permeated the air, but all Maggie could concentrate on was getting away from her pursuers. Plus, she was disgusted with the slick feeling along the bottoms of her feet sliding inside her soaking wet shoes.

"Maggie, wait!" Grisham called to her. Maggie wanted to reach the other side of the park where she'd come out not far from her car, but the grounds were so congested she bumped into more people, leaving a symphony of *"Ouch!,"* *"Excuse me!,"* and *"Watch where you are going!"* in her wake. Ahead of her, Neal popped into view and quickly started to walk toward her. Maggie stopped and turned to head in any other direction only to see Mike eyeing her as he breathed heavily and wiped some sweat from his brow. He looked at Maggie and didn't blink or shift his gaze as he also closed in.

Maggie didn't see any avenue open for her to

run. There was no familiar face among the bunch. But before she had a chance to do or say anything, a loud voice cut through everything.

"I told you if you ever came around near my stand again, I'd make an example of you!" It was Lou of Lou's Better Beef. Maggie hadn't realized she was just a couple yards from his stand, and he hadn't forgotten that Mike and Neal tried to steal his profits.

"Forget about it, Lou," the man in the parks uniform said. He appeared at Lou's side, trying to take his friend by his arm and reign him in. His hand barely made it halfway around the beefy part of Lou's bicep. No one could stop this bull if he decided to charge.

"We don't want any trouble from you, sir," Grisham said and looked Lou closely in the eyes. "We're all friends here. Tell me, do you have a troubled heart? Do you need a friend?"

"You aren't my friend. I've had about enough of you and your group. God only knows how much you've stolen from the people out here trying to make an honest living. And you preach to me?" Lou stepped around his grill and met Grisham halfway.

"Lou, calm down. You don't need this right now," Mr. Parks Uniform said.

"I assure you that no one in my care is a thief," Grisham said. Maggie recalled Angel telling her that thieving was a big part of proving how dedicated the members were.

"Oh, yeah? Those two are." Lou pointed a thick finger in Neal and Mike's direction. They were smart enough to hang back. Maggie was stuck in the middle.

Grisham didn't look at his men. Instead, he focused on Lou and started to walk toward him. Maggie didn't understand everything Grisham was saying, but his words reminded her of the character Wormtongue in *The Lord of the Rings*. He repeated what Lou was saying and nodded like a snake trying to hypnotize its prey. There was something sinister in the way he was validating Lou's complaints while at the same time pulling Lou's justified aggression from him. Grisham was utilizing a technique that Maggie had read about in more than one of the books on cult leaders and New Age so-called prophets.

"We're hard-working people in this town," Lou hissed.

"You're hard-working people, yes," Grisham replied.

"Don't you condescend to me, pal!" Lou barked.

"Lou, you gotta stop. Remember what happened before. Come on. You! Get out of here! They aren't worth it, Lou," Mr. Parks Uniform begged. He looked very worried about his friend and whatever Grisham was saying didn't seem to have the same effect on him.

"Who is condescending? Not me," Grisham volleyed back.

"I know what you're trying to do, and it isn't going to work." Lou clenched his fists as he took another slow step toward Grisham. By this time a small group of people had stopped to watch, but most people were unaware that a confrontation was taking place. At first, Maggie was sure that Grisham's technique would at least calm things down. But Grisham had to have the last word. It would be his last.

"You don't understand what I'm trying to do, sir. It is beyond your current state and…" That was all it took. Lou pulled back and punched Grisham in the face. Neal and Mike wasted no time rushing to their leader's side. Mike turned and was about to give Lou a taste of his own medicine, but Mr. Parks Uniform got in between the men.

Maggie stood and watched with both hands covering her gaping mouth. The punch was not what made her stand there frozen in shock. It was what Mr. Parks Uniform had said.

"*Remember what happened before.*" Could it be that Lou had lost his temper with Echo? Lou did describe him earlier and said he made an example of him, or someone. Maggie shook her head as two uniformed officers came running up to the scene.

After the wallop it looked like Lou had dished out, Grisham was able to get back to his feet. Only a small trickle of blood came from the corner of his mouth. He wiped it with the back of his hand and glared at Lou. All that love and peace business wasn't there anymore. The leader of the Greater Society of Atonement was not prepared to have someone withstand his hypnotic personality.

"Come on! You'll get more of the same!" Lou shouted as poor Mr. Parks Uniform tried to push him back. With both his hands on Lou's huge barrel chest, the police got between them as Mike was now ready to fight. Shouting and threats ensued, but before long the police got the parties involved to opposite corners.

"They tried to rob me before! And I put an end to that right quick! Why should I think they wouldn't try again? I remember your faces! Each one of them!" Lou ranted on and on, unwilling to work with the police at all. It didn't take long for the officers to put the cuffs on him and start to escort him through the crowd as they ordered Grisham and his followers to meet them at the police station to file charges.

"I'm afraid we have to," Grisham said.

"But what about Echo? And the pawn shop?" Neal whispered. "And what about her?" When he pointed at Maggie, she felt her blood boil. What did he mean by "what about her"? What *about* her?

There were enough witnesses to put all the blame on Lou for starting it, even though Grisham obviously antagonized him. But that didn't matter. Maggie went up to the officers as they walked a slowly simmering Lou, who still managed to mutter his side of things.

"Officers! Those men were chasing me. Mr. Lou was just trying to help," Maggie pleaded. They barely slowed down to talk to her.

"Chivalry isn't dead, but it doesn't give the man the right to punch another one in the face," one of the officers said.

"But that guy back there asked for it. He was needling Lou." Maggie wasn't sure what she was hoping to accomplish. If Lou tossed Echo off the Hickory Creek Bridge, wouldn't it be better that Lou be locked up? But if he didn't do it and the members of the GSA were more involved than they were letting on, this meant they were going to look like the martyrs.

"Ma'am, if you want to make a statement you can meet us at the police station," the other officer said. Lou stopped walking, turned to Maggie, and gave her instructions through clenched teeth.

"It doesn't matter. Just go home." He didn't know who Maggie was or why she'd be trying to help him. His words made her stop in her tracks and watch as they led him away. His shoulders were hunched, and he continued to mutter as he walked. No one was listening to him.

Suddenly, Maggie remembered the reason for all the hoopla and whirled around. Grisham and his men were nowhere to be seen. She squinted into the crowd and didn't see them anywhere. They had been so determined to talk to her, but now they disappeared. Maybe with the police now involved they'd get cold feet and leave town and Angel and, for that matter, Mr. Lou alone for good. The smell of the beef still cooking was still in the air.

At Lou's Better Beef stand, the man in the parks

uniform was busy packing everything up. He was shaking his head and muttering, too. Maggie carefully walked up to him. He had been at the Copper Tower Hotel with Lou too. They must have been good friends. He had to know something about Lou and his relationship with the GSA.

Chapter 17

"The guy just doesn't know when to quit," the parks worker grumbled.

"Have you known Lou a long time?" Maggie asked, making the man jump slightly. "I owe him. Those guys were following me, and I'm thankful he stepped in. I'm sorry for what happened though."

"Yeah, Lou was my best friend since high school. Always had a bit of a hot head. But come on. Those people tried to take his money. I was with him when they did it." The man wiped his hand on his pants and extended it to Maggie. "Calvin Rice."

"Maggie Bell." She shook his dry, rough hand.

"I tried to tell him to just let it go but just seeing

those people set him off. He's right. Who knows how many other people they've ripped off," Calvin said. "We followed those two punks who were just here to the Copper Tower Hotel. All the way Lou was calling them out, warning people that they were pickpockets and thieves. He was right. Call me whatever you want."

"Do you know what Lou did the first time they tried to rob him? You'd said, remember what happened last time. Did something happen with those people?" Maggie asked.

"Yes. It did," Calvin said as he stuffed napkins back inside the bag they came in and the same with the plastic utensils. "Lou hasn't been thinking straight since his wife left him. I told you he had a hot head. Not that he'd ever raise a hand to a woman. Never. Especially her. But the man she was running around with?"

Maggie swallowed hard as she listened.

"You can't blame a man for getting violent when someone is birddogging his woman. Evelyn had packed her bags and left the same night that scrawny punk tried stealing his cash box. He had no idea what he was walking into." Calvin continued to tell how Lou had been going on three or four days barely sleeping. He said he'd been meeting Lou at the booth when things were winding down and closing for the night. When he described the man Lou taught a very severe lesson, Maggie felt her heart lodge in her throat. That man was Echo.

"I don't know who that punk thought he was, getting in Lou's face when he caught him red-handed. He's lucky he was able to keep that hand." Calvin shook his head.

"Maybe the guy was on drugs or something?" Maggie prodded.

"He had to be. He looked like he'd been crying or was totally strung out. Anyone challenging Lou had to have some screws loose. That was for sure."

"Was there a girl with him?"

"No. No, not that I remember," Calvin said. "But the young man did make a queer comment that he wasn't afraid to die because love lived forever. I remember that because it stopped Lou for a split second while he scratched his head. If only that punk would have stopped there. He reached for the cash box right in front of Lou, and that was all it took. *Bam!*" Calvin punched his right hand into his left palm.

Maggie flinched. Echo never struck her as a

genius in any realm of life. And the way he thought he was clever, she believed that he would have been so brazen as to take someone else's money right in front of them, as if his bright green eyes would somehow distract them from the crime he was committing. She was sure that his eyes were what that captivated her sister. Angel had that whole *his eyes were the windows to an old soul* mentality when it came to Echo.

"Lou punched him?"

"Sure did. I had to get between them. I worried that Lou was going to go after me for stopping him. But fortunately, a couple of the locals who know us separated everyone without the cops being called. That kind of luck doesn't last," Calvin said. "I'm sorry. Did you say those guys were following you?"

"Yeah. They are a strange group, like a cult that my sister was involved with. She doesn't want to be part of it anymore, but they don't seem to know how to take no for an answer," Maggie replied.

"That explains their weird slogans. All this talk about love and peace while they are stealing your money. I just don't get it. Fair Haven is a nice little town, but it does have the tendency to attract some real strange people. I don't mean your sister..." Calvin shrugged.

"No. You are right. And she can be strange. But she's my sister, and these guys keep hounding after her. She was, um…married to the man that Lou punched in the face."

"Really? Sorry about that," Calvin said, squinting as if he might have felt part of the pain inflicted on Echo.

"Don't be. I get the feeling the guy was not a good egg. You know, he showed up dead." Maggie watched Calvin's reaction. He froze for a second, looking down at a huge cooler of beef before bracing himself against the edges and letting his head drop forward. Then he looked back at Maggie.

"Are you kidding?"

Maggie shook her head and told Calvin that the police had found him at the bottom of the Hickory Creek Bridge just the other day.

"That was when he crossed Lou," Calvin said. "This doesn't look good."

"Do you think Lou had a chance to follow this guy and take his frustrations out on him?" Maggie asked carefully.

"I'm not with Lou twenty-four hours a day. I didn't talk to him that night. But he was annoyed the entire day. Especially because this fellow had the gall to spout weird poetry about love and death. It stuck in Lou's craw all day and didn't seem to ease up when he locked up the booth." Calvin shook his head. "He's just going through some stuff. I don't think he could have killed anyone. Not on purpose."

"You're sure there was no girl with him when Lou confronted him?" Maggie asked.

"No. He was alone. Although I do recall those two numbskulls who jumped in today were not far in the background. I believe they were lookouts or ready to cause a distraction if things went too far. It was all planned. That I believe. And poor Lou was the pigeon they thought they could hoodwink. He made an example of that boy, that's for sure."

Maggie felt bad for Lou and his situation. It brought to mind the image of her sister in Joshua's shirt. Was she going down that same ugly path of envy? Was it worth it? She shook her head and reached out her hand.

"Thanks, Calvin. I'll make a statement at the police station in Lou's favor. You are right when you say that Grisham taunted Lou. I hope Sheriff Smith will take the side of a local rather than some snake oil salesman from out of town. I've had enough of this group slinking around and making trouble," she said as Calvin quickly shook her hand but was too distracted getting everything packed up.

"I'm going to have to post bail. This is a mess," Calvin muttered. He gave Maggie a quick nod as she left.

Chapter 18

When Maggie reached the sidewalk, she felt like she'd just emerged from the jungles of the Congo. The air was cooler and fresher, and the shadows were gone from the bright sun overhead.

"Hey!" she heard Angel call from behind her. When Maggie turned around, she saw Angel still in a pair of jeans and the big, baggy shirt that Maggie was sure was Joshua's. She didn't look like herself, but of course, she didn't look bad. Nothing could make Angel look bad. Maggie smiled and dashed up to her sister, wrapped her arms around her, and squeezed her hard.

"Where have you been? No, wait. I don't care

where you've been, Angel. I'm just glad you are safe," Maggie said and stroked her sister's hair.

"Mags, I'm in trouble," Angel said.

"Let's not talk about it here. Come on. Let's go to the bookshop and…"

"I just came from there. This is Joshua's shirt because…"

"Angel. You are beautiful and smart, and Joshua would be a fool not to see all the beautiful things about you. I'm happy if you guys are together and…"

"Okay, Mags. Now you are the one who has been smoking the wacky tabacky. Joshua is a nice guy but not my type. First of all, he's too old," Angel said in a huff.

"He's my age," Maggie replied with eyebrows pinched together.

"Exactly," Angel replied. She rolled her eyes, which looked tired but playful.

"Okay, look. If you go to my house, will you stay there until I get done with work? It's a really busy time, and I can't leave the bookstore for any longer than I have. Joshua needs me and…"

"He certainly does," Angel replied. "More than you know."

"What? What does that mean?"

"I'll wait for you at your house. Then, we need to really talk," Angel said as she wiped her running nose on the back of her hand.

"Promise?" Maggie asked as she pulled her keys from her pocket.

"Promise," Angel said.

Maggie handed her keys to her sister and hoped she'd keep her word. The girl had been so irresponsible about coming and going that Maggie was sure she'd come home to find an empty house and a note that said something like *fell in love with a clown from the parade. Gone off to join the circus.*

Quitting time couldn't come fast enough that day. No matter how busy they were, and they were bank-breakingly busy, it felt like each minute took five more minutes to pass. Finally, Maggie rushed home and found Angel had kept her word. But her sister didn't look well as she stood in the doorway waiting for Maggie. Her red-rimmed eyes and pale complexion made Maggie's heart break.

"What's the matter? Please don't tell me Grisham was here," Maggie said as she hurried to her sister's side.

"No," Angel replied.

Maggie gently pushed Angel into the house and

shut the front door, slipping each lock into place. "Did you do it, Angel? Did you kill Echo?"

"No, Maggie. I didn't kill him. But I'm glad he's dead." Angel swallowed hard. "I didn't tell you everything that happened between the two of us. It was such a mess."

Angel took a seat on Maggie's small scratchy couch and began to cry. The story was one Maggie never dreamed she'd hear from her sister. Angel had always seemed like such a strong, vivacious woman, someone who would walk away from someone who didn't treat her right. But she was so much more complicated than that. She was so much more than just a pretty face, and it was only after this tragedy that Maggie was coming to realize it.

"Echo caught up with me that night. He had been crying, and I knew that he was in a bad place. He'd become addicted to some medication he was taking, and he was trying to quit smoking too. Funny how Grisham told the rest of us that all we had to do was offer up our whole selves to the spirit of light and we'd have every ailment cured. Every harmful habit or nagging worry would be gone just like that." Angel snapped her fingers.

"Angel, what habit did you have that needed to be dispelled? Aside from dating weirdoes, you seem pretty stable to me." Maggie tried to make Angel laugh and succeeded. But after a brief smile, Angel's waterworks started and didn't stop.

Angel told a story that Maggie had heard before on television and on talk shows. A young woman fell in love with a man and then realized he wasn't what she thought he was.

"It was good at first, Mags. Sure, if I look back now, I could tell there were little things that should have tipped me off that Echo had a problem. He couldn't sleep. No matter how hard we worked during the day, and we worked hard, he just couldn't find sleep." She wiped her eyes. "We were supposed to rely on nature and Grisham's instruction for anything we might need. So Echo went to him for help. At first Grisham seemed to really try to help Echo. But as soon as he found out about Echo's family, everything changed."

"What about his family?"

Angel looked down and worried a hangnail on her thumb. "They were very wealthy. Very wealthy. All I know is they made money whether the stock market went up or went down. I don't know how that works. All I know is that it never made a bit of difference to me what Echo's family did. You have to believe I did love him…at first."

She went on to describe how Grisham and some of his men researched everyone who wanted to join the Society. "That was how they knew about you. And they would use that knowledge to keep some of us under control. Maggie, there were a lot of good people in the society who liked what it was all about. They liked the work, the beliefs. They didn't seem scared or lost at all. But when I learned they were keeping Echo there because he had a fairly large trust to tap into, it made me feel sick. Like when they told me to steal. They were telling Echo to do the same thing from himself and his family. And the problems he had sleeping became worse."

"Obviously. In his gut, he probably knew he didn't belong there," Maggie replied softly so as not to disrupt Angel's train of thought.

"That's when they gave him the Halcion. It didn't take any time for him to get addicted to that stuff. Plus, he was trying to quit smoking. If you are having trouble sleeping and trying to kick the nicotine habit at the same time, you have to expect something to give. He became violent," Angel said. "Maggie, I'm so embarrassed."

Maggie scooted closer to her sister and put her arm around her, soothing back her hair with one hand while gently squeezing her shoulder with the other.

"What was wrong with me, Mags? We didn't grow up in a bad place. Why did I let this happen? Why didn't I walk away from him the first time he called me stupid? The more I tried to help, the harder it got. The meaner Echo became. Until finally, Mags, I had to find you and get away. I had to." Her eyes indicated there was still more to the story.

"Angel, did he hit you?" Maggie asked quietly. When Angel's only reply was to cry harder, Maggie didn't need her to say another word.

"When I tried to get Grisham and his men to help, to talk to Echo and straighten him out, they told me it was my job to keep Echo happy. But that was impossible, Mags. You have to believe me."

"I do, Angel. Of course, I do. Did this start before or after you got 'married'?" Maggie made the air quotes with her fingers but quickly resumed embracing her sister.

"After. I thought we were going to be one of the original families at the commune. You know how there had to be some people who set the example. I thought that was going to be us. We were happy and having fun. I was so naïve that I was sure we could accomplish anything with the love we felt for each other. But it wasn't enough, Mags. It wasn't even close," Angel said. "Not when you've got people actively working to undermine what you are doing with your mate. The person who should have been at the bottom of that bridge was Grisham. He's a bad, greedy man and somehow gets people to follow him. My gosh, I did." A fresh wave of tears rolled down Angel's cheeks. "I'm so ashamed of myself."

"What do you have to be ashamed of, Angel?" Maggie snapped. "Why, you are nothing but kind and accepting, and you are brave and my gosh, Angel. I always wished I was more like you. You just seem to be willing to give anyone the benefit of the doubt. Heck, I don't trust anyone." Maggie's words weren't as eloquent as she'd hoped. Angel pulled back and looked at her like she'd just sprouted a head of cauliflower out of the top of her head.

"I always wished I was more like you. You've got such a big vocabulary, and no one would ever try to pull anything over on you. You're too smart for that. This would never happen to you, Mags. You'd never be so stupid," Angel said with a smile as her voice hitched in her throat. "I should have never let Echo talk bad about you. I'm so sorry about that."

"It's okay. We were both a lot younger. I've been called worse things by better people than him. Livelier people too." Maggie shrugged.

"Oh, Mags! That's in very poor taste." Angel knew she shouldn't laugh, but that was what made it all the funnier. After a quick break from the tears Maggie asked the hardest question. What happened the night Echo died.

"He had gotten cut off from his family's money. I was the only one who knew about it. So, Echo was stealing anything he could get his hands on. Anything. Including from me," Angel sighed.

"Your amethyst ring."

"How did you know?" Angel gasped.

"I have ways of finding things out." Maggie would wait to tell her sister how she snuck into the hotel room, how she listened and got a good idea about Echo's money and why the Society was so interested in getting Angel back.

"Yeah. He went to pick up his prescription at the drugstore, and they didn't fill it. He went nuts. He would have gone more nuts if he knew it was me that had called and cancelled that prescription. I had it sent to a drugstore in Odell. It can sit there forever for all I care," Angel said. "I was broken up with him and starting to feel like myself again. But he insisted I go with him because he wanted to talk to me. The truth is, Maggie, I had some things I wanted to say to him."

"I'll bet you did," Maggie replied.

"We went to the pawn shop, and that was where I saw he had my ring from dad. You remember the one with the amethyst in it? I was crushed because he knew how much that meant to me. He took the money and didn't even offer me an explanation or anything. It was as if I was just supposed to accept what he'd just done. I started to cry but held it back. There was no way I'd miss his reaction at the drugstore. But when we got there, and he didn't get his stuff, he went nuts. I was in trouble. I should have come home right then. I should have come right home. But I didn't. I should have, but I didn't."

Chapter 19

Maggie braced herself to hear that Angel had accidentally pushed Echo off the bridge or that she'd hit him with a rock and pushed his body off the platform. Whatever it was, she would stand by her sister and get her the help she'd need. For Pete's sake, she was abused. She had every right to defend herself.

"Echo was a mess. He was begging me to go with him and telling me that he just needed to walk, and he'd feel better. But when I saw we were going toward the bridge, I just got a crazy feeling inside. He was trying to hold my hand and tell me how beautiful I was and that he was so glad I was his wife. Just a lot of stuff all at once. It was like he was telling me all this stuff before it would be too late."

Angel stopped, looked at the floor, and licked her lips.

"Whatever it is, Angel, you did what you had to," Maggie said.

"Maybe I am a horrible person for kicking him when he was down, but I told him we were done." Angel swallowed. "I let loose. Mags. I told him everything that had been bottled up in me for so long and even took a couple of cheap shots. I hate to say it, but it felt good. He stood there like he was witnessing a UFO land in front of him. Just letting his mouth hang open while I told him I was leaving and never coming back. I thought it was going to be easy. I thought I'd built up enough strength. But when he sprang at me, I was no match."

"Did he try to... do other things to you?" Maggie trod lightly as she spoke to her sister. No sudden movements or loud accusations. She felt like she was trying to coax a red-breasted robin into her hand. She let out a long breath she'd been holding when Angel shook her head.

"Echo kept talking about being together forever. He tried to pull me toward the bridge. I thought he was going to toss me right over. Instead, we fell to the ground, and I was kicking and scratching and clawing at everything around me to get away. That was why I looked the way I did when I got home."

"Oh, Angel. You should have let me call the police."

"I didn't want you or the police involved. I just wanted to be done with him. I thought I was when I got away and ran all the way here. Well, I took a few wrong turns. Everything looks different in the dark." She clicked her tongue and shrugged.

"So, when you left Echo, he was alive?"

"Very much alive. Very angry and bitter and alive," Angel said. "My hand to God, Mags. I didn't do anything but break up with him."

Maggie swallowed and squeezed Angel's shoulder. "You don't have to worry about anything. I'll help you. We'll get to the bottom of this, and once all the facts are out there, you'll be free and clear."

"I won't be free until Grisham and his goons leave town. They don't plan on doing that without me." Angel shook her head again. "Why? I don't have anything to give them."

Maggie sat up straight and lifted her chin. "I know why they won't let you go."

Angel leaned back and looked up at her sister. Her right eyebrow arched with interest. Angel's eyes dried, and she smirked slightly. "Mags, you look like the cat that swallowed the canary. What have you been doing while I've been running for my life?"

Maggie explained how she snuck into the hotel rooms, hid behind the curtains, and heard Mike and Neal's conversation. She couldn't help but feel proud as her sister stared at her, eyes wide with disbelief and her mouth hanging open.

"You did what?"

"It doesn't matter what I did. What matters is what I heard. I think they want to keep you in the fold because you might be entitled to Echo's money. But they don't know his family cut him off. The whole Society might be in for a rude awakening. I think it's about time we involve the law, and I'm not taking no for an answer."

Once more, Angel shook her head.

"I can't believe that you did something so dangerous. So sneaky. You realize you could have been arrested. Maggie, are you crazy?"

"Do you think I'm just going to let someone pin a murder on you? Or drag you off to be some kind of sacrifice to a snake god for a cult to get your inheritance? You don't know me all that well, Angel." Maggie smirked proudly.

"That's for sure," Angel said before throwing her arms around Maggie's neck and squeezing her like she'd done when she was little. Maggie hugged her back as tightly as she could. Just as she was feeling confident not just in their relationship but with what happened to Echo, Maggie remembered seeing Angel in Joshua's shirt. Her heart twisted, and the old feeling of envy tried to worm its way between them. She pulled back and looked at Angel.

"So, I saw you this morning at the bookstore before it opened. You didn't come home last night. Why were you in Joshua's T-shirt this morning with no pants on?" Maggie asked.

Angel shook her head and started to laugh. "I was mad at you, but I was on my way back to the house when your landlady spotted me. I don't think anyone can get away from her with a simple yes or no answer to anything."

"Mrs. Peacock wants details. Yes or no aren't details." Maggie nodded knowingly.

"Yes. So I made up a quick fib that I suffered insomnia and was hoping to walk off my anxiety, so I'd be able to sleep tonight. Well, she's an insomnia expert. If only I knew her before Echo got hooked on his insomnia pills." Angel shrugged.

"Mrs. Peacock is an expert on finding things out," Maggie said. She stood up, got a glass of water from the tap, and took a sip before handing it to Angel, who gulped down the rest.

"Well, she invited me into her house. What a house." Angel went on to describe the beautiful interior that Maggie was more than familiar with. "Can you believe she's on a fixed income? With all that beautiful furniture and knick-knacks. My gosh."

Maggie nodded. Not a soul in all of Fair Haven didn't know Mrs. Peacock was on a fixed income.

"Did she tell you that?"

Angel nodded then continued with her story. "She was telling me about how you had been a good tenant and that she saw how much you suffered after Mr. Whitfield's death. She said he was practically your only family and that you kept so much to yourself in the bookstore. She couldn't understand how someone so pretty and smart could hole up like you did. I'm sorry, Maggie. I didn't know any of this."

"What could you have done? It was just Mr. Whitfield's time." Maggie smiled sadly as she thought of her old boss. He'd been gone for a while but not long enough for Maggie not to get teary-eyed when she thought of him. She sniffled and wiped her nose on the back of her hand like she'd seen Angel do.

"I could have been a decent person and offered to help you with anything you needed," Angel said with a huff.

"What? And miss out on all this drama? You've got to be off your rocker," Maggie teased, smiling away her tears for Mr. Whitfield.

"Anyway, Mrs. Peacock and I talked for a long while. About you and me and our family. I told her we'd had a tiff and about the Society, but I didn't go into details. I told her it was a club and that I'd had enough. That was when she told me about the dramas revolving around someone named Donovan. Do you know who she was talking about?" Angel asked.

"Do I? Mrs. Donovan is Mrs. Peacock's best friend and nemesis. Those two compete over which one of them is more competitive. They can't live without each other. But go on." Maggie sat next to her sister and listened.

"Mrs. Peacock said Mrs. Donovan was a terrible gossip and that if I were to keep roaming around the yard, she'd have it spread all over town by morning. So she invited me to just stay in the main house until the next day while things cooled off between you and me." Angel chuckled as she stood from the kitchen table and went to the cupboard to retrieve a bag of chocolate chip cookies.

"How did you know those were there?" Maggie asked as she got up and poured them both some milk.

"I do know you *a little*." Angel wrinkled her nose and rolled her eyes. "The next morning Mrs. Peacock was up making fresh squeezed orange juice. It was delicious. So she gave me two big cups to take to the bookstore. One was for you, and one was for me. She thought it would make a nice peace offering, and so did I.

"I went to the bookstore and tried to be cool in front of your boss by juggling two huge OJs while helping him get the newspaper in front of the door right when a cat decided to jump up in the window and scare the daylights out of me. I was drenched. And sticky." Angel pinched her lips together and tilted her head to the right. "Joshua had that apartment upstairs."

"That was where Mr. Whitfield lived before he passed," Maggie said.

"That was what Joshua said. He told me to go wash up and gave me a T-shirt while he took my clothes to the laundromat. He's a really nice guy for someone so old," Angel ribbed.

"He's not collecting Social Security or taking his teeth out at night. My gosh. Give the guy a break," Maggie said.

"You sure seem sweet on him. Are you guys an item?" Angel asked.

"What? He's my boss, Angel. No. Nothing. Nothing is going on between us. Why would you ask that? Did he say something? Because I never said anything of the sort. No way. That's nuts." Maggie said.

"Hmmm… if I may quote Shakespeare. Ahem. Methinks thou dost protest too much." Angel peeked at her sister from beneath heavy eyelids. "Admit it."

"There's nothing to admit." Maggie ate a cookie and took a sip of milk.

"Sure. If that's the case, I won't tell you what he said about you," Angel replied.

"Right. He said something about me. Are you kidding? He practically tripped over himself the second he saw you. So did half of the guys in town as soon as they found out I had a sister. Like usual," Maggie said.

It was funny. When she said the words out loud,

it was as if her envy fell away like a bulky, itchy sweater she could finally shed. Why wouldn't she want people to notice her half sister? She was a good person. Young and adventurous and even a little silly. It was okay to be that way. Maggie decided if her own personality was more introverted that was because she liked it that way. She did. So why not enjoy Angel's complementary personality?

Maggie listened to Angel talk about some of the fun things she'd done while she was away, things that didn't involve Echo or the Society or anything painful or ugly. By the time they had finished the cookies and milk and gotten ready for bed they'd laughed, cried, and laughed again. It was the best time Maggie had had with Angel in her whole life.

That night, Angel crawled into the bed next to her sister and gave a wide long yawn as soon as her head hit the pillow.

"Tomorrow we have to go to talk to Gary. He'll know what to do about everything," Maggie said and crossed her fingers that Angel wouldn't put up any kind of fight.

"If you really think that would be best." Angel yawned again.

"I do. You know Gary is a really smart guy. He's

not going to jump to any conclusions without looking at everything. It will be all right. I can just feel it." Maggie nodded as she settled into her own pillow. Angel didn't reply. When Maggie looked over, she saw Angel had already fallen asleep. She said the words, but Maggie couldn't help but worry. Would Gary believe that Angel didn't do anything to Echo? Would he understand that she was desperate to get out of a dire situation? Only with the sunrise would she find out. She listened to her sister's steady breathing next to her. Angel had fallen asleep immediately. Maggie lay awake for a short while, trying to set aside any doubt that the police would believe Angel's story. She believed it. Every word of it. That was for sure. Maggie believed her sister.

Chapter 20

The bookstore was closed for the last day of the Fair Haven celebration. The fireworks that were scheduled for the evening had the whole town buzzing with excitement. The park was clear of all the vendors to make room for people who were already staking out their spots for the sky show.

"This looks like so much fun. Everyone out here for the day enjoying the sunshine and nature and conversation," Angel said as they walked among the people who were spreading blankets on the grass and setting up small barbeque pits and picnics. This would be an all-day affair for most of them.

"This looks like a long time to spend outside

with only a port-o-let at your disposal," Maggie replied.

"Why would *that* be the first thing that crosses your mind?"

"The question should be why *wasn't* that the first thing to cross your mind," Maggie wrinkled her nose and looked at her sister before they both chuckled. Then a calm quiet settled over them as they walked along the sidewalk. They were headed to the police station. Angel was ready to tell the authorities what had happened that last night Echo was alive. She was also ready to tell them about her involvement with the Greater Society of Atonement and express her concern about what they were doing in town and their usual way of going about things. Would she be held for the thieving the group was doing? Would she have to pay for their sins? Had they already beat feet out of town?

As soon as that thought crossed her mind, Maggie saw the familiar glare of Grisham approaching. He had a swollen bruise on his chin from the decking Lou gave him. She didn't have to say anything to Angel. Her sister immediately took her hand and squeezed it. Maggie's heart hardened toward the men as they approached because she could feel Angel's hand tremble. How dare they scare her little sister this way.

"Angel. We've been looking for you," Grisham said as Neal and Mike moved to surround the women as they'd done to Maggie the other day through the park.

"Hold it right there!" Maggie shouted and pointed her finger at the men. They stopped more out of shock than intimidation as the scattering of people on the scene looked on.

"I wasn't talking to you, Margaret," Grisham said with a smile that dripped condescension. "Just give me five minutes, Angel. I just want to talk to you. I know you are missing Echo. He was your husband. You owe it to him to talk to me."

"You don't owe anyone anything," Maggie replied, squeezing Angel's hand.

Neal and Mike stepped closer to them as they scanned the faces of the people who were casually watching the scene before continuing their celebration of the last day of the centennial.

"I don't have anything to say to you," Angel replied. Maggie had never seen her so nervous. Her hand was still shaking even with the bright sun shining and people walking past.

"That's okay, Angel. I just need you to listen,"

Grisham said and took half a step closer. "Can you spare five minutes for someone who really loves you? You know your sister doesn't really care about you. You told me how different you both were and how Margaret always tried to change you by insinuating you weren't smart enough, weren't conservative enough. You were never enough. Do you think that has changed?"

"Oh, for Pete's sake. Are you really trying that old game?" Maggie pinched her lips together and rolled her eyes. "That's brainwashing 101." But just as the words left Maggie's mouth, she felt Angel's hand loosen in hers. It didn't matter. Maggie squeezed tighter.

"Weren't those the things you confided in me, Angel? Didn't you spend many nights in my tutelage looking for relief from the guilt your sister had placed on you? Don't be afraid. You can tell her now that you don't need her anymore. You're home, Angel. Your home is with us." Grisham reached out his hand, but Maggie stepped in front of Angel and shook her head.

"If you want Angel, you'll have to go through me. And any of the people on the street that see three men lunging for a young lady. I might not be big, but I'm betting you won't get far." Maggie squared her shoulders.

Grisham and his men looked around. There weren't many people, and most of them were no longer paying any attention to the discussion on the sidewalk. But there were enough that if a scene was made, the Society members were outnumbered.

"I won't have to lunge for her. She'll come with me herself. Won't you, Angel?" Grisham smirked as he stared past Maggie and into her sister.

"Maggie?" Maybe no one else noticed, but Maggie heard the fear in her sister's voice.

"He can't touch you," Maggie said as she pushed up her glasses and waved her hand at Grisham as if he were nothing more than a pesky fly.

"But he's right. I did say those things about you. And worse," Angel muttered.

"Oh no! Angel! How could you?" Maggie said as if she had gone to the William Shatner school of over-acting. "Right, because in the history of sisters, we were the only ones who didn't like each other for a spell. Where is your family, Grisham? Do you have any brothers and sisters? Where are your parents? Mike? Are you related to him? Neal? I didn't think so."

Grisham's expression made it clear that he was getting angry. "Angel, we don't have time for this."

"No. *We* don't have time for this." Maggie still held tight to Angel's hand. "We're on our way to the police station. In fact, Sheriff Smith is waiting for us. Angel will be giving her statement about what happened to Echo. And I'll be making a statement in defense of Lou's Better Beef that you three instigated him into a fight. So you are welcome to tag along. But if the sheriff has to come looking for us, you boys might find yourselves tarred and feathered before he runs you out on a rail."

Grisham smiled at Maggie and chuckled. But she could tell he wanted to call her every name he could think of.

"What did you do to Echo, Angel?" Grisham asked before tilting his head to the right.

"What? Nothing!" Angel panicked.

"You don't have to answer him," Maggie snapped.

"You did it, didn't you? You pushed him off the bridge. It's okay. You were distraught over the way he was treating you. I only wish you would have told me about it sooner. I would have stepped in," Grisham taunted.

"I did tell you," Angel muttered. Maggie

couldn't believe her vivacious, brave sister was being chipped away right in front of her.

"You didn't tell me until it was too late," Grisham said, shaking his head pitifully. "You tried to do things without me. Now look at the trouble you're in."

"Oh, no! This is going to stop right now! You aren't in any trouble, Angel. We know what happened, and we're going to the sheriff now. So help me God if you try to stop us," Maggie barked.

A large shadow fell over the sidewalk from behind Maggie and Angel. All Maggie saw was Grisham, Neal, and Mike's eyes as they looked up above the women's heads. Maggie turned around and was never so happy to see the intimidating form of Patrick Cusic standing behind her.

"Are you girls having a problem?" Patrick asked, his sleepy eyes glared at Grisham.

"Not anymore," Maggie replied as she started to pull Angel away. "Make sure they don't follow us. They've been doing that for days."

All Maggie could hear was Grisham trying to reason with Patrick for a few seconds before Patrick told him in no uncertain terms to be quiet and leave before things got ugly.

"Did you see that? I'll tell you all about Patrick

later. I never thought I'd be happy to see that guy. But what a lifesaver. Come on, Angel. Let's get to the sheriff's and... what's the matter?" Maggie asked when she realized Angel was crying.

"I'm so embarrassed. I told Grisham things in confidence and...oh Maggie. I didn't mean to talk about you like that and..."

"This has got to stop. You didn't do anything wrong. We are siblings. Siblings fight. They call each other names, and they gossip to their friends about them. Jeez, even the sisters in *Little Women* fought, and they were darn near perfect. That's why it's fiction. Get over it, Angel. I have." Maggie huffed and pulled her sister along in the direction of the police station.

They walked in silence for a few minutes. Angel sniffled back her tears and wiped her nose on the back of her hand. Finally, Maggie spoke.

"Did you see how I stood up to those guys?"

"Yeah. To be honest, I was shocked," Angel said with a chuckle.

"Didn't know your big sister could be that tough, did you?"

"Nope. I sure didn't."

Chapter 21

"Lee, how many times do I have to tell you? The pink form is for the state. The yellow is for the file. I know you are kind of new at this sheriff-ing, since you've only been the law in Fair Haven for twenty years, but if you could make an effort that would be great," Gloria said from behind her desk near the police station's front door. A vanilla scented candle glowed happily on her nearly spotless desk.

"Didn't realize I'd asked for sass with that question," Sheriff Smith replied without any facial expression. He was a barrel-chested man with a gleaming bald head who was slow to burn but near impossible to put out once ignited. He took his job protecting the folks of Fair Haven seriously and liked that his town was a safe place filled with families and friends. But then there was the occasional death that sparked an investigation like Echo Mann had done.

Maggie held the door open for Angel to walk in. She couldn't help but feeling that Angel would change her mind and not say a word to anyone about what had really happened that night with Echo at the bridge. All Maggie could do was hope and wait.

"Hi, Maggie Bell. What can we do for you today?" Gloria chirped happily as she smiled at Maggie and looked her sister up and down.

"Hi, Gloria. This is my sister Angel. She needs to talk to the sheriff," Maggie said quickly. She pushed her glasses up on her nose, pouted, and stepped back for Angel to look awkwardly at Gloria and then the bulky man who wore the badge.

"Oh, okay. What do you need to talk to the sheriff about, honey?" Gloria asked. Her wrinkled forehead and straightened spine let Maggie know once again that someone was shocked the two of them were sisters. They looked nothing alike, but the way Angel squinted just then before answering Gloria was like watching herself in a mirror. So maybe they weren't hugely different but had only been apart so long they didn't have a chance to see what they had in common.

"I was with Echo before he died," Angel said softly. "I don't know who killed him, but I can tell you what I do know."

"Is that so?" Sheriff Smith said and ran his finger beneath his thick mustache, turning up the ends like the lawman in any Louis L'Amour novel.

"Yes, sir." Angel sighed and nodded.

Sheriff Smith walked over and held the gate open for Angel to enter the area that contained all the officers' desks. "We can talk in my office, ma'am. Follow me."

Once Angel was out of the room with the sheriff, Maggie looked at Gloria. "I'd like to make a statement too. I was a witness to the altercation between Lou's Better Beef and those guys from the Society of Greater Atonement. It wasn't Lou's fault."

"That was a big mess. A big bull of a man like that doesn't realize his temper is his enemy, not the people around him," Gloria said.

"That may be. Gloria. But those men egged him on. They taunted and needled him, and with all he's going through, something was bound to snap," Maggie said.

She told Gloria what Calvin had told her. There was no telling by Gloria's expression if what Maggie had to say would make a lick of difference. But that didn't matter. If nothing else, it might alert the sheriff that Grisham and his men might be all love and kisses on the outside but rotten on the inside. They didn't really want to help Lou any more than they did Echo or Angel.

"Well, you'll have to wait for one of the officers to get back. They'll take your statement," Gloria replied. "Why don't you help yourself to a cup of coffee and have a seat. I think Gary will be back shortly."

"Where is he?" Maggie asked and squinted as she tugged at the hem of her blouse.

"Odell. The body of that man found at the bottom of the Hickory Creek Bridge had to be sent there because our medical examiner has been gone fishing for the past two weeks."

"Oh," Maggie replied as she hurried over to the coffee pot and poured herself half a cup of joe. She took a seat at the desk she knew was Gary's and held the cup with both hands. Not a single sound came from the sheriff's office. Maggie hoped that was a good sign. But just as she was about to relax in her chair, the front door burst open.

Grisham was alone and looked angry. Maggie's first thought was that Patrick had done something and Grisham would press charges on him along with Lou. But he didn't say that when he came up to Gloria's desk.

"Mr. Grisham, why am I seeing you so soon?" Gloria asked. Maggie looked at him from beneath pinched eyebrows.

Just as he was about to speak, he saw Maggie sitting there. His face turned an angry shade of red before he started talking. When he pointed at Maggie, she nearly choked on her coffee.

"That woman had a man come and threaten my life and the lives of my associates," Grisham said. "I want to press charges against her and the man."

"Maggie Bell had someone threaten your life?" Gloria asked before turning around to look at Maggie and then back at the serious gray-haired man standing in front of her. "Mr. Grisham, I have to ask if you've been drinking since we last talked."

"What?" he snapped.

"I've known Maggie for years, and well, are you sure you've got the right person?"

"Oh, I get it. An outsider has a complaint, and it must be that they are the troublemaker. You can't imagine anyone from this town being uncivilized or downright violent. Can't expect a fair trial to take place in Fair Haven, can I?"

"Mr. Grisham, I would suggest you watch your tone with me or else…" Gloria stood from her desk, and the silver pistol in the holster on her thick hip gleamed proudly from her side. "We will be having some trouble. Now, you'll have to wait until one of the officers returns to file an official complaint. Who is the other party involved?"

"Patrick Cusik," Maggie offered before taking a slow, careful sip of her coffee.

"Patrick Cusik? Ha! He threatens at least eight people a day and has yet to act on any of those threats. Mr. Grisham, did you feel your life was truly in danger?" Gloria chuckled.

"I'm glad you find this so humorous. I'm sure that you have had to brush a lot of incidents under the rug because of your position in this office," Grisham said in a low voice, like he was trying to hypnotize Gloria or put some kind of spell on her. Maggie's heart jitterbugged in her chest as she anticipated Gloria's response.

"My position in the office?" Gloria asked.

"Being the secretary who keeps everything going

but can be replaced easily if she doesn't follow the men's rules. It's a common theme. I see it all the time. You know I'm right," Grisham cooed. "Women need to be reminded they are equal and that…"

"Ha ha! Mr. Grisham, you might dazzle a few young girls who don't know any better with that kind of blubbering. But it doesn't work on real women. But thanks for the laughs. Have a seat, Mr. Grisham."

Maggie didn't hide her smirk. Instead, she held her chin up high, feeling superior, since Gloria had unknowingly included her in the group of *real women* who didn't fall for his spiel. She went to take a sip of her coffee just as Grisham was about to start protesting, but both were cut short when Officer Gary Brookes came walking into the office looking annoyed.

When he saw Maggie, his annoyance immediately turned to worry. "Maggie, what are you doing here?"

"I need to talk to you about Lou's Better Beef," Maggie squinted.

"Excuse me! Officer! My life was threatened, and I need to file a complaint." Grisham stood up with his hand raised like he was in a classroom.

"Sit down. I'll get to you in a minute," Gary barked.

"What's the news on Echo Mann?" Gloria asked.

"Suicide," Gary said. He stood next to Maggie, who was sitting next to his desk and nearly choked on her sip of coffee.

"What?" she said with a gasp.

"Yup," Gary said as he pulled the paperwork from his pocket that he'd rolled up from the medical examiner's office. "Cause of death, suicide. Apparently, Echo Mann who had a history of abusing prescription drugs for the past seven years and had Halcion in his system combined with just enough Prozac and OxyContin to cause a severe bout of confusion and depression. At least, that was the conclusion the ME came to," Gary said.

"Did he have a prescription for any of these things?" Maggie asked. She knew from Angel about the Halcion and the way it made people act. But didn't Prozac calm a person down? And what the heck was OxyContin used for?

"He did not as far as I could tell. Someone had to give it to him who didn't know the side effects it could cause when combined with other drugs," Gary said as he looked at Grisham. "You wouldn't happen to know where he got his hand on some Prozac and OxyContin, would you?"

Grisham shook his head, but Maggie wasn't convinced.

"His body was busted and broken, and a severe blow to the head was what killed him. He had six broken ribs. His left lung was punctured. Both legs were broken. Cuts and scrapes, of course. But if it makes anyone feel better, aside from the voices in his head, he probably didn't feel much of anything or even be aware what he'd done," Gary said.

"What do you mean voices in his head?" Grisham asked. He looked very nervous.

"The ME said that the combination of drugs probably caused not only a bout of depression but also suicidal thoughts. He might still be here if he hadn't combined the two," Gary said.

"You look like you've got more on your mind, Gary," Gloria said. "What is it?"

Gary looked at Maggie and swallowed hard. "I'm not sure how to tell you this."

"What is it?" Maggie forgot she was holding a cup of coffee and sat stone still looking up at Gary. His eyes held an angry glint that was not directed at her. He wore the look someone might have after realizing they'd been cheated or violated in a way they didn't know had even happened.

"It's about your half sister," Gary said.

"What about Angel?" Maggie set the cup on Gary's desk and stood up. There was movement out of the corner of her eye, but she didn't flinch.

"During the course of the autopsy, the ME removed Echo's shoe from his right foot. Inside it was a note," Gary said. "I made a copy. The original has to stay with the evidence. We will have to confirm it was his handwriting, but if it was, there was a very sinister plot in motion."

"What does this have to do with Angel?" Maggie squinted and pushed her glasses up out of habit.

Gary looked at the paper in his hands. Reluctantly he gave it to Maggie to read.

"Oh my gosh, he really addressed this to '*cruel world*'? It's starting like a Bugs Bunny cartoon," Maggie scoffed before continuing. Her gesture might not have been compassionate, but she couldn't tolerate bad writing.

However, her flippant attitude became one of surprise and anger.

. . .

"*By the time anyone reads this we will be long gone. Love cannot last in this place of destitution and depravity. We tried to blossom and grow together, but no matter how hard we tried, there were obstacles at every turn.*

"*Angel, such an appropriate name, will lift me to heaven with her as we enter into paradise together.*

"*Some of you may be left wondering how this could be true. But you'd never understand a love like ours. It will exist long after all the world has dissolved into dust.*

"*We will say goodbye and leap into eternity, hand in hand, our hearts racing as one in the most perfect act of love.*"

THE NOTE WAS SIGNED by Echo, and he also wrote in Angel's name. Maggie felt a queasiness settle in her stomach. This was why Echo was pulling Maggie toward the bridge. *He* was going to murder *her*.

"My gosh." Maggie clutched her belly. "She came home that night covered in mud and scratches. If he'd gotten a better grip on her... if he'd pulled harder or managed to get the upper hand...she'd be..."

"But she isn't. Maggie. She's fine. She's safe. Echo did this to himself," Gary said sternly, as if the words needed to be harder for them to penetrate her head.

"I thank you, Miss Bell, for coming to talk to me," the sheriff said as his door finally opened. Angel stood there, and it was obvious from her red eyes and the way she wiped her nose again on the back of her hand that she had been crying. The sheriff handed her a tissue form a nearby desk that she balled up in her hand and didn't think to use.

"Thank you, Sheriff," she mumbled then looked at Maggie, sighing in relief. But Maggie and Gary's expression were enough to cause her to stop. "What's the matter?"

Maggie swallowed hard and wrinkled her nose as she handed the copy of Echo's letter back to Gary. She didn't want to hold it anymore. Maggie felt that maybe somehow the filth of the words and the intent would seep into her fingers and make the nausea stay in her forever.

"Uh, Sheriff, we got the report back from the medical examiner's office in Odell in regard to the death of Echo Mann," Gary started. He repeated almost everything he had told Maggie and Gloria and disclosed the gruesome plans Echo had made for Angel and himself.

"He left it all in this note that was in his shoe.

The ME found it when she was conducting, well, you know," Gary said.

"What does the note say?"

Gary swallowed, read the photocopy of the note, then told her what he concluded. Angel didn't move for a couple of seconds. Then she turned and looked at the sheriff.

"Is it my fault?" she asked.

"Of course not," Maggie chimed in.

"There were drugs in his system that contributed to his behavior. Plus, based on the letter and the fact it was in his shoe and that he had to have time to write it makes me tend to believe that he was going to kill you one way or another. You're lucky to be alive," Gary said. Maggie looked at him. He bit his lower lip and looked like he'd wished he could have done anything but tell Angel these ghoulish details.

"Didn't you say he was trying to pull you toward him?" Maggie said as she walked up to Angel. "Didn't you say you ended up fighting and rolling on the ground?"

Angel didn't answer.

"Angel, I went to the scene. There were clear, precise shoe imprints that matched Echo's, showing he walked or maybe even ran to the edge of the bridge and leapt." Gary took out his notepad and read everything he'd scribbled down. Maggie wondered what kind of story all those little notes told about him. "Where his body was found was not consistent with someone who accidentally slipped and fell. It didn't even match someone who was pushed or thrown from the edge. As far as the evidence went, this was a suicide. Echo launched himself off the edge. Had he landed in the water, he might have lived or even been swept away and never found. But because of all the hot weather we'd been having, he missed the shoreline. Fell on dry dirt. I have to say, Angel, I'm not trying to speak ill of the dead, but I'm glad for your sake there was only one body."

"That still doesn't say where he got the Prozac from," Angel said. "He wasn't taking that. I'm positive."

Maggie leaned over to look at Grisham only to find he was no longer there. He was the movement out of the corner of her eyes that she'd noticed before. Not only was he no longer interested in filing a complaint on Patrick Cusik, but he was not concerned with what the Fair Haven police had to say about the death of one of the members of his association.

"He was spotted coming out of the drugstore. But there are some people I'd like to talk to. One of whom just slipped out the door," Gary said casually.

"Aren't you going to go after him?" Maggie pointed toward the door.

"There's no hurry. Half the streets are blocked off for the fireworks. They'll be driving in circles for hours before they realize I'm right behind them." Gary looked at Maggie and gave her a wink. She smiled and crinkled her nose with excitement.

"Miss Bell, I'll ask that you not leave town just yet. We may need to corroborate a couple of things with you as the rest of the report on Mr. Mann is completed," Sheriff Smith said firmly.

"I wasn't planning on leaving, Sheriff. Not yet," Angel said. She looked at Maggie and took a deep breath that made her shoulder rise then settle with relief.

As they left the police station, Maggie and Angel heard Gloria put out an all-points bulletin on Grisham and his men and anyone else affiliated with the Society.

"Do you think they'll catch them?" Angel asked.

"Of course. This is Fair Haven's finest. Why?" Maggie twisted her face as if she were really concentrating on Angel's question. "Are you scared?"

"A little. It doesn't take anything to find out where someone lives. They might come to Mrs. Peacock's place and what if they try to hurt her," Angel asked, kneading her hands.

Maggie knew that Mrs. Peacock put on a stellar act of a shrinking violet when she was really more than capable of taking care of herself. The woman didn't have a twelve-gauge shotgun within reach because she was easily intimidated.

"Mrs. Peacock will be okay. She's got a really good security system. Plus, Mrs. Donovan watches her house almost continuously. Nothing is going to get past those two," Maggie said, chuckling.

"What if he comes after you?" Angel said softly.

Maggie looked at her sister. They were walking down the sidewalk just across from where the fireworks would be ignited once the sun went down. More people had set down roots in the park, and the smells of charcoal and lighter fluid mingled with the smells of burgers and hotdogs.

Small golf carts hummed past with volunteer members of security in the seats. Giggling children ran happily across the streets, which were wide open, closed to all traffic. Off in the distance the sound of amateur fireworks could be heard, popping off or whistling in the air.

"He wouldn't dare. Besides, he's just a guy who thinks he can worm his way into a person's head with flowery talk and pressing hot-button issues that most people have. Rough childhoods, or broken hearts. Who hasn't experienced those things? My gosh." Maggie huffed. "I'm on to him. Besides, I think Mr. Patrick Cusik has a soft spot for me. I'll just tell him to make an appearance."

"That guy was a giant," Angel replied.

"You should hear him when he yells at people. He was actually being kind of nice today," Maggie said, shrugging.

"Maggie? Was it my fault Echo jumped?"

"What? Why would you think that?" Maggie snapped.

"He came to me. He was asking for help, and I didn't even think there might have been something else going on," Angel said, her bottom lip starting to quiver.

"Angel, he was sober enough to write a suicide note for the both of you. He had plans of living out that '*Don't Fear the Reaper*,' song and you were Juliet to his Romeo. What do you think would have happened had he asked you to jump with him and you said no? Do you think he would have said 'Well, okay, honey? I'm going to kill myself, but you don't have to come with me. I just thought I'd ask'?" Maggie scratched her head and then her chin, jutting out her lower jaw like a yokel.

"Don't make fun, Mags. He had a problem. I just didn't know how bad it was." Angel wiped her eyes but didn't break down. Maggie was sure Angel felt some relief under all of this because she no longer had to look over her shoulder and worry he was coming after her. But still, Angel did love him. No matter how odd Maggie thought that was, it was true.

"Yeah, *he* had the problem. Not *you*. You did the right thing. Angel, do you even realize what the alternative outcome would have been? You would have been at the bottom of the Hickory Creek Bridge. We would have never had a chance to talk. A chance to get to know each other better like we have. I would have missed out on every-thing. Everything, Angel. The thought makes me sick to my stomach." Maggie snapped her words, but she was more shaken up by what could have happened to her sister than she was letting on. She felt it was her job to take care, since she was older and had more experience. Now more than ever she felt part of a family. Not like with Mr. Whit-field who was the sweetest man she'd ever known and who was more than just a father figure but a real guardian angel. For the first time, Maggie felt a special bond that she and Angel shared. They had the same blood. How much closer could two people get? Even if it was only from their father, it was there, and it was precious. So a strange feeling of protection had settled over Maggie. How could she share her experience with Angel without coming across as condescending or like a bossy-britches?

You really haven't had more experience than Angel. She's been experiencing things in real life. You've been experiencing them in books. Her conscience decided to butt in after being quiet for a long time. She wished it would stay quiet.

Come on and admit it. The girl has been out in the world her whole life. You've been buried in books your whole life.

"But I like books," Maggie whispered.

"What was that?" Angel asked.

"Nothing. Just thinking out loud," Maggie looked around at the festive scene around her and inhaled. "What are you going to do now?"

"I'm not sure. I've got to break this news to Echo's parents. Like with you, we barely spoke to them. Since I was his wife, I feel I should be the one to tell them," Angel said.

"Don't you want to leave that to the police? They have experience in that sort of thing, and his parents might blame you. They might not have any idea about his drug use. Don't put yourself in the line of fire if you don't have to, Angel," Maggie said.

"I've still got some time to think about it. Gosh, I wish I could just forget about everything for a little while. Just to rest my brain. It feels like Echo has been echoing in my head for... ever." Angel snickered.

"I have a good idea. How about we go see the fireworks tonight?" Maggie said. Sitting in the dark and in the grass with mosquitos and strangers around her was the last thing she wanted to do. But she felt the need for a distraction too.

"That sounds like fun. Can we?"

"Sure. What the heck." They walked the rest of the way home.

Chapter 22

Maggie and Angel decided to make a real affair of the fireworks show. They picked up cheese and crackers and fresh fruit, and although Maggie wanted Doritos with onion dip, Angel insisted on kale chips with hummus.

"You'll like it, I promise," she said to Maggie's pinched face and rolling eyes.

"You would have liked Doritos and onion dip," Maggie replied.

"Maybe. But no one who talked to you would have. Did you ever think that maybe that little concoction is why Gary hasn't asked you out?" Angel teased.

"Gary? He's the deputy of police!" Maggie

retorted as they drove as close as they could get to the prime fireworks watching area. They ended up parking a dozen blocks away, but the evening was cool and pleasant for July, and lots of people were bustling about.

"I know exactly who he is, and he's sweet on you," Angel replied.

"I think you are confusing sweet with mildly fascinated like I'm a bizarre lab creation," Maggie said. "Besides, he's not who I'm… never mind."

Angel gasped. "You're sweet on someone else? Who? Tell! Tell!"

"I'm not sweet on anyone," Maggie said, grumbling.

"Okay, well in this tiny town there can only be so many fellas to choose from. Patrick Cusik?" Angel said, trying not to laugh.

"Oh my gosh! No! Even if I was, the laws of physics would prevent us from ever being able to even kiss normally. *No!*" Maggie replied with a wrinkled nose and grin on her face.

"Well, Sheriff Smith is married. So we know it isn't him. And I don't think it is the man who runs the pawn shop," Angel continued.

"Can you stop? The fact you are even entertaining the thought of these people is not just amazing to me but almost offensive. And I don't think you deserve any fresh fruit. You can gnaw on your kale as punishment."

The conversation continued as they made it to the park. At the edge of the tree line was a wide open space filled almost entirely with people on lawn chairs and blankets, waiting for the show to start. Maggie and Angel found a small spot off in the corner that had one tree that obstructed some of the view, but they were okay with that. It wasn't really the fireworks they came to see. They just wanted to be sisters for a little while.

"That leaves only one person. So, does he know?" Angel smirked.

"Who? I'm telling you there isn't anyone who I am interested in. I don't have time for that sort of thing." Maggie spread out a blanket on the ground before taking a seat. Angel arranged their food and handed Maggie a bottle of water.

But just as they were about to relax and enjoy themselves, a familiar face crept out of the darkness.

"Angel?" he whispered from the bushes before emerging. Grisham didn't look anything like he had before. His peppered hair was mussed, and his clothes looked wrinkled and dirty.

Maggie crawled in front of her sister and pointed at him.

"You stay away from her or so help me, I'll..."

"I'm not here to hurt her. You should know that. Angel, have I ever hurt you? You know I haven't. In fact, I've taken care of you. You don't know this, but I protected you from Echo. If I hadn't given him what he needed, heaven knows what he would have done to you," Grisham said, spilling his guts desperately.

"You are supposed to be a leader," Angel spat. "We were all doing so well at the Society until... something happened. Echo's family cut him off. Oh my gosh, you were using his money to fund that place. It wasn't all of us working together. It was you stealing from your members. I didn't have any money, but I had Echo. That was why you pushed us to get married. That was why you wanted me to stay. There was a chance he'd leave if I did, and then you'd be left with nothing."

"That's so stupid," Maggie chimed in. She couldn't help herself.

"You have to come with me, Angel. You aren't going to throw away our bond for this person who was never there for you. That was what you told me. You told me she was no sister of yours. That she didn't care and that she was jealous of you and that she meant as much as a stranger walking down the street." Maggie could feel Grisham's poison working on Angel

"You're right. I did say those things about Angel," Maggie piped up. "She's as odd as a three-dollar bill. We don't have anything in common. Nothing but one thing. We have the same blood. So you can either leave right now and get a jump on the police, or we start screaming and get every able-bodied man in the vicinity to come running."

"See how she's trying to control you, Angel? Even after you've become a woman, she wants to control you," Grisham purred. He did have a rather velvety voice, but Maggie was immune to it. In the dark, she was afraid it might work its magic on her sister.

"What do you want from me?" Angel whined.

"Come home with me. You belong with the Society. That's who loves you. That's who cares about you. Would we have come all this way if we didn't?" Grisham replied.

Maggie looked around nervously, but she didn't see Neal or Mike anywhere. Was Grisham alone? Had they bailed on him now that the law had gotten more involved in Echo's death?

"Where are your sidekicks?" she asked.

Grisham took a step closer and extended his hand. "Come with me, Angel. Before it's too late. Before your sister poisons you against your real family."

"Oh, that is really pathetic! You've reached a monumental level of pathetic now," Maggie snapped.

"She's right about that," said another voice from the darkness, one that Maggie recognized instantly. Gary and another of the uniformed officers stepped out of the shadows.

Grisham seemed to shrink in front of them and lost control of his tongue. "I haven't done anything wrong. There is no crime in accepting donations from a wealthy member of our family or his spouse."

"So that was what he wanted you for," Maggie said to Angel. "You were the key to keeping Echo happy, and without Echo, you as his wife might have been entitled to a pretty penny of inheritance." Maggie pointed at Grisham. "You are one sick puppy!"

"Mr. Grisham. We'd like you to come peacefully to the station for some questioning. Now, all these nice people are here trying to have a good time.

Please don't make a scene, and please put your hands behind your back," Gary said calmly and respectfully.

"What am I under arrest for? I didn't do anything to Echo or Angel. He killed himself because of drugs. You said so yourself," Grisham said in a voice that lost all of its smoothness and became a jittery whine.

"Seems that you are in violation of your parole," Gary said. Although it was hard to see in the dark, Maggie was sure he had a huge grin on his face. "You aren't supposed to cross state lines, nor are you supposed to associate with known felons. Neal Minchill has a real problem with keeping his hands to himself, doesn't he? Several charges of theft. A couple of assaults. A sprinkling of carjackings just for show. You really need to pick better members of your *family*."

Right then and there, the smooth-talking, manipulative leader of the Greater Society of Atonement began to sob. It was the most unnerving thing Maggie had ever witnessed.

"This is what we were afraid of?" she whispered to Angel, who shook her head in disbelief. "If he starts wailing, I'm going to be left with no other choice than to slap him," Maggie continued.

"Ladies, enjoy the fireworks," Gary said as he let the other officer slip the silver bracelets on Grisham and lead the blubbering man away.

"Do you have time to sit for a while?" Angel asked. "*Maggie* and I would like it if you could. Now that you're done with Grisham."

"I'd like that, but a policeman's paperwork is never done." He smiled, and despite the darkness, his eyes stayed on Maggie the entire time. After he left, there was an awkward quiet from Maggie's side of the blanket.

"You mean to tell me you can't tell he's sweet on you?"

"Angel, if you use that term one more time, we are going to have a good, old-fashioned sibling fight. And just remember, I'm older than you, so I can probably beat you," Maggie replied as she squinted and wrinkled her nose.

"Yeah, sure, four-eyes. Anything you say," Angel replied then giggled.

"Oh, real mature. Are you sure you weren't adopted?" Maggie snapped back.

"I wish I was," Angel added, making them both laugh.

Their conversation flowed from that point on, and as the fireworks began and the oohs and aahs commenced from the people around them, Maggie and Angel enjoyed their time together like two sisters should.

"So, are you really serious that you're not interested in anyone in all of Fair Haven? There's got to be someone," Angel said as she finished a bite of cheese.

"Maggie! Maggie! Over here!"

Maggie's back stiffened and her mouth went dry.

"Oh, hi, Joshua!" Angel waved in his direction. Maggie looked and saw him quickly coming over as though ducking enemy fire or walking under the spinning blades of a helicopter.

"I didn't think you girls were going to be here. I would have saved you a better space than this. You guys are seeing mostly trees," he teased. "Do you want to come and sit with us?"

When he leaned back and pointed at the place he'd come from, Maggie nearly choked. There, sitting on the blanket, was Joyce from the bank in a barely-there tank top and short shorts. Maggie felt like her bones wanted to escape from beneath her skin.

"No. We're good here," she said quickly and tugged at the hem of her sweater. She'd let Angel talk her into wearing a sundress but didn't dare leave without a sweater over her shoulders in the old-fashioned style buttoned at the collar. A bright American flag pin in rhinestones lay over her heart, but no one could see it in the dark.

"Thanks again for the use of your shirt the other day," Angel said.

"Did you tell Maggie about that? You can tell you guys are sisters. The clumsiness is hereditary. Maggie's had a couple of epic spills too." Joshua teased.

"Very funny. I quit," Maggie said without smiling, making her sister and Joshua laugh even harder.

It didn't escape Angel's notice that Maggie looked away from Joshua and twisted her hands nervously.

"Joshua, I think the fireworks are about to start," Joyce called. She never stood from her place on the flannel blanket to come and say hello.

"Your date is waiting," Maggie said with a crooked smile just before pushing her glasses up on her nose.

"You know Joyce from the bank," Joshua said innocently.

"Yes," Maggie replied and went to give an

obligatory wave, but Joyce was too busy looking through the picnic basket next to her to notice.

Joshua turned to make a comment, but Joyce didn't notice him either. He cleared his throat and bent down on one knee between Angel and Maggie.

"If you change your mind, we've got some food. I brought some fried chicken and a couple dozen sodas, and I made some brownies, but they got a little burnt," he chuckled.

"You cooked all that for you and Joyce?" Maggie asked, unable to hide the disappointment in her voice. He'd never so much as offered her anything more than coffee from the café.

"Actually, I bought the chicken at the store. I had thought a couple more people were going to show up, but it turned out that only Joyce could make it," Joshua said. "So please, help yourself if you get hungry. I have strawberry soda. Didn't you tell me once that you liked strawberry soda, Maggie?"

"I don't remember," she muttered and shifted on her blanket.

"You do," Angel chirped . "I forgot about that. She does love strawberry soda. When we were kids, that was what she'd have for all our family parties.

If I remember, you remember. My gosh, how long has it been since you had one?"

Maggie shrugged but smiled as the thought that her half sister remembered some tiny detail about her sank in.

Joshua nodded then turned to his cooler and popped the lid. He reached in and grabbed two cans before Joyce could protest. Joyce's eyes were narrow slits.

"Here you go. For old time's sake. Angel, you strike me as a root beer kind of girl. Hope that's okay," Joshua said.

"You got me pegged. Thanks, Joshua."

Before Maggie could utter a thank-you, the music started, and one single firework shot off in the air, sending the crowd into whoops and applause. Maggie popped the top of her can of soda and took a sip. The sugary sweet taste of candy strawberry brought her back to a less compli-cated time. She enjoyed her life. But something about the taste and the bubbles made her feel bold.

"Cheers, Angel." She held up her can.

"Cheers, Mags." Angel clunked her can with her sisters, and they both took a long sip and let out a satisfied *ahh* after they swallowed.

The sky was illuminated with bursts of amazing

colors and patterns perfectly in synch with the patriotic themes being played over the loudspeakers. The night was perfect. Off in the distance Maggie could see a couple of stars. When the sky lit up, she saw all the couples and families together, pointing and smiling. A couple of couples kissed, seeing fireworks of their own.

"He's looking at you," Angel said, leaning closer to her sister.

"Who?" Maggie wrinkled her nose.

"Who? Joshua, that's who," Angel said.

"He's here with Joyce. The most horrible woman in all of Fair Haven." Maggie kept her eyes focused on the fireworks and didn't dare look in Joshua's direction.

"Yeah, he said there were supposed to be more people. You know what that means, don't you?"

"Yes. That I'm not the only one who doesn't want to be around Joyce." Maggie chuckled at her own comment.

"It means that was the only way she could get him to come out with her. My gosh, Mags. With all the books you read, you mean to tell me you haven't read any romances with conniving women and their methods? That's skank behavior 101." Angel nodded.

"How do you know?"

"I'm your younger sister. I'm not a nun," Angel replied. "Besides, if I were interested in Joshua and you were my competition, I'd be pulling out all the stops too." Angel patted her sister's hand.

Maggie shook her head, clicked her tongue, and took a sip of her strawberry soda. Only once did she sneak a peek in Joshua's direction—at a time that just happened to be when he decided to do the same. She quickly adjusted her skirt and looked back up into the sky. Her heart raced.

Suddenly, the colors bloomed brighter, the music sounded even more inspiring, and the smells of her strawberry soda and the cool grass and the hint of smoldering charcoals were intoxicating. Angel mentioned a memory of fireworks when they were young that triggered a long giggly conversation between the two girls. It was a wonderful evening.

Chapter 23

"It feels like you were barely here, and now you're leaving," Maggie said as she stood outside Mrs. Peacock's home with Angel waiting for a cab.

"You are a liar. I know you, Mags. You are happy to have your solitude back." Angel smiled. "Believe me, I'd stay longer except that now I have to deal with these lawyers and Echo's mother and father. They are just devastated by what happened. I feel so bad for them."

"At least they can take comfort in knowing the men who fed Echo's addiction are in custody. Grisham and Neal won't be pulling in any more victims for their fake society," Maggie added.

"I can't believe I fell for their scam." Angel shook her head.

"You wanted to be happy. That was all. There is no crime in that," Maggie said. A quiet settled between them as they looked in the direction the cab was supposed to come.

"I'm happier now than I ever thought I would be. I've got my sister," Angel said, making Maggie's eyes fill with tears. She took Angel's hand and squeezed it.

"Oh, none of that. She's not leaving to join the Foreign Legion. She's just going to Boston to sign some papers, visit some in-laws. Maybe they'll even cut her a big check as an inheritance," Mrs. Peacock said as she brought out two glasses of fresh orange juice onto the porch. "You'll come visit us again, won't you, Angel?"

"Of course I will, Mrs. Peacock. I'm sure you'll see quite a bit of me once all this red tape is cut through," Angel said and took a drink. Maggie did the same. The sweet juice was ice-cold and delicious.

Just then, Gary pulled into the driveway in his squad car. He got out and proceeded up the walk. "Good morning. I think the cab right behind me is for you." He smiled at Angel but stood next to Maggie.

Before she could reply there appeared a yellow cab in the driveway.

"No long good-byes and weeping," Angel said. Now her eyes were filled with tears that flowed down her cheeks.

"No. No weeping," Maggie said. "That's for damsels in distress who are lost in the woods or women who have been jilted by a scoundrel or knave."

"You read too many books." Angel laughed.

"You don't read enough," Maggie. She hugged her sister tight before whispering in her ear, "Come see me again soon."

All Angel could do was nod. She quickly got into the cab and slammed the door shut. She waved to everyone, wiping her nose on the back of her hand just as Maggie did the same. She stood at the edge of the sidewalk until the cab disappeared.

"Your sister is very nice," Gary said.

"Yeah. She really is."

"But she's not at all like you."

"No. That's why everyone likes her. She's got a way with people," Maggie replied.

"She's got a way with people. But you are one

of a kind," Gary said. Before Maggie could say anything there was static then chatter on his radio. A fender bender on Main Street.

Gary left without another word, leaving Maggie smiling.

About the Author

Harper Lin is a *USA TODAY* bestselling cozy mystery author. When she's not reading or writing mysteries, she loves going to yoga classes, hiking, and hanging out with her family and friends.

For a complete list of her books by series, visit her website.

www.HarperLin.com

Made in the USA
Las Vegas, NV
16 January 2023

65694032R00152